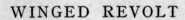

WINGED REVOLT

THE MACHINE WENT SLIDING DOWN

Frontispiece.

WINGED REVOLT

BY

ERIC WOOD

AUTHOR OF
"WINGED MOUNTIE" "REBEL SKIES" ETC.

LONDON
THE ACE PUBLISHING CO.

MADE AND PRINTED IN GREAT BRITAIN BY PURNELL AND SONS, LTD.
PAULTON (SOMERSET) AND LONDON

CONTENTS

LIST OF ILLUSTRATIONS

WINGED REVOLT

CHAPTER I

SKY DUEL

"What the blazes is the matter?" Ted Rapson turned from the theodolite with which he was making a survey across a river, one of numerous obstacles to be taken during the building of Liberia's first railway. Rapson was chief surveyor-engineer to the British firm, which had obtained, in face of much international competition, a concession over a large tract of country, and he was working on the railway which the Government had insisted should be driven. As he turned, the man running towards him stopped the shouting which had interrupted Rapson's work. He was Jim Leader, one of the large number of white men engaged on important jobs.

He stopped, panting, before Rapson.

"Trouble, Ted!" he gasped. "Monrovia. Got——"

"Reckon it would be trouble to bring you all hotted up like this!" Ted grinned. "But take your time. Monrovia's a long way off!"

Leader took deep breaths, standing there with the copper ball that was the African sun ablaze above, with the jungle through which toiling natives had cut a way after the scrub had been burnt, spreading on either side, and with sounds of metal clanging on

9

metal, the clatter of excavators making a hideous
cacophony. There was an engine chuffing to get up
steam while its wood-burning furnace swallowed in a
few seconds what sweating men had taken hours to
hew out of the forest. The empty wagons behind the
engine were to be taken down to Monrovia where
supplies of all sorts, materials of all kinds, were to be
had.

"Telegraph's cut, Ted!" Leader blurted out at last.
"At least, I reckon that it was cut while I was taking
the message, which ended abruptly. I tried to contact,
but there was no answer."

"Natives, maybe," said Rapson, looking at the line
of poles that stretched away down the length of the
new railway. It was no unusual thing for the wires
to be cut; the original natives of the republic of freed
American slaves had a fondness for copper wire. "Is
that all, Jim?"

"No!" Leader answered crisply. "There's trouble
at Monrovia, Ted! Revolt! Jameson down there got
through to say that Executive Mansion was being
attacked by armed men. President Adams Coolidge,"
he grinned as he recited the sounding names, belonging
to a Negro whose forbears a few generations ago were
slaves in the cotton-fields of the Southern States.
"President asks," he went on, "if we can send down
help, and can you go down in the 'plane—with dynamite?"

"Eh, what's that?" snapped Rapson. "We're
not soldiers, Jimmy!"

"I know we're not," Leader admitted. "But
Jameson says things are confoundedly serious. We

know there's been a lot of unrest lately. Jameson says that fellow Kebreau's on the rampage again!"

"Kebreau, eh?" exclaimed Ted Rapson. He had heard of, although never seen, Kebreau, an erstwhile official in Monrovia who had been cleared out of office when President Adams Coolidge had, because of corruption, been compelled to make a bloodless purge. The result had been that Kebreau had gathered round him a band of discontented sacked officials, who, backed by young Liberians fired with zeal for a political ideology, the ultimate significance of which they knew practically nothing, had tried to carry out a *coup d'état*, with the intention of setting up a totalitarian Government. The attempt had failed. Kebreau had disappeared, leaving many of his dupes to face the music.

The railway contractors had been told, afterwards, that had Kebreau succeeded, one of the first moves by the new Government would have been to try to cancel the concession. Kebreau had seized on the then unpopularity of the projected railway which the Liberians considered a waste of money that could have been better spent down at the coast. The average Liberian was not over-interested in the development of his country, and, after all, the interior was mountainous jungle in which lived savages. That these savages might conceivably be the direct ancestors of the Liberians, whose forefathers had been snatched in many a blood-thirsty slave raid, counted for nothing.

"Yes, Kebreau again!" Leader said in response to Rapson's exclamation. "Jameson was saying something about 'planes when he was cut off. At least, that was all I got, and I was unable to connect again. I gathered from Jameson, by the way, that Mr. Darcy authorised the request for us to go down."

"That's different!" Rapson knew that it was his duty to obey Andrew Darcy, the firm's representative in Monrovia. "Let's go!"

They hurried to the temporary buildings that were headquarters. As they went, they snapped out orders to men, who in turn dashed along the line and in all directions to warn the workers to go and listen to something Rapson had to say.

"I'll do the talking, Jim!" Rapson said. "You hustle along and get the 'plane fuelled up. I'll send Dawson over with a case or two of dynamite."

"Okay!" Leader darted off in a new direction. Rapson, when he came to the engine, jumped on the footplate and bellowed above the noise:

"How soon before you can start, Harding?"

"Ten minutes, sir," the driver answered, and Rapson told him what was afoot.

"Take three wagons down, Harding," he said. "One will carry men, the others wood—that'll save stopping so often on the way. Hey, you!" he roared as a stream of men went past, heading for the offices. "Fall to and load a couple of wagons! And work like the dickens!"

The men, Liberians, and natives recruited in the country through which the railway was passing, hurried to obey. Rapson sprinted to the offices, outside which large numbers of men were waiting, wondering what was afoot. Rapson told them. Some of the men were whites, and he called for volunteers amongst them.

"I want only enough to use the firearms we've got," Rapson said. "Oh, there you are, Dawson!" he broke off, as a broad giant of a man, one of the white foremen, appeared. "Get two cases of dynamite and some fuses over to the 'plane. Leader's there. You did some flying during the War, didn't you?"

"I'll say so!" was the grim answer. Dawson was now a little over forty, but he could not forget those days when, as little more than a schoolboy, he had torn across the skies of Flanders.

"I'd like you to go with me, Dawson," Rapson told him.

"Sure!" and Dawson's face broke into a wide grin. Life, it seemed, was promising a diversion from ordering black fellows about. He hurried from the spot, and Rapson looked at the men who had stepped forward in response to his appeal.

"All the durn lot!" he murmured. "But I can't take 'em all, because some of the Liberians up here may not be altogether loyal. Some of the natives, too, might take it into their heads to make trouble if there weren't enough whites left. I'll have to take a mixed lot!"

He wanted forty men. His eyes darted from man to man, his finger jerked out, pointing at this one and that. These stepped out to one side, white men and coloured.

"The rest get back to work!" Rapson ordered.

"I'm trusting everybody to carry on while I'm away. Let me say this: I reckon your job depends on how this thing works out."

"Long live the Government!" an ebony-faced man, wearing what remained of a frockcoat, flung the rim of a top-hat into the air. The cry was taken up enthusiastically.

Rapson hurried into the office, tried to contact by telegraph with Monrovia, but failed. The selected men came in, and were given firearms: rifles, revolvers, automatics, a couple of big elephant guns, and an old muzzle-loader which one of the Liberians had brought up with him and, as was the rule about weapons, deposited with authority.

As he was handing one of the elephant guns to a white man, Rapson shook his head.

"No," he said. "I reckon I'll take it with me, and that one, too!" He signalled to the white who had the other powerful firearm. "I'd forgotten that we may need guns in the 'plane. Take my revolver instead." He tossed the latter weapon over to the white, who looked as if he preferred it to the elephant gun.

"Diamond!" Rapson thumbed towards one of the whites, who stepped forward. "You've been a soldier, haven't you?"

"Sergeant, sir," was the answer.

"Then you're in command," Rapson told him. "The plan is to get into Monrovia and do the best that's possible. If you can, go in on foot, and try to take by surprise the men who, as far as we can gather, are attacking Executive Mansion. But I'll have to leave everything to your discretion. I'm going down in the 'plane, with Dawson and Leader. Good luck, all of you!"

"Luck to you, sir!" came the chorus as Rapson elbowed through the little crowd and hurried over to the clearing in which stood the Leopard Moth that had proved such a good servant to him. For a long time before ever work was started on the building of the railway, Ted Rapson had flown over Liberia, taking aerial-survey photographs. They had been used to help to a decision regarding the exact route the railway should take. Then, again, the Moth had been of excellent service as a swift means of travel between railhead and the coast. Injured men, too, had been flown down to Monrovia, and urgent supplies been brought up. Those had been errands of peace, but Ted Rapson frowned as, nearing the machine, he realised the character of the present mission.

"The devil of a business," he muttered. "Darcy must know what he's doing, asking us to butt in. Anyway, I hope so! All set?" he asked, as he reached the 'plane. Leader's helpers looked as if they had finished bringing up petrol drums and Jimmy was pouring in oil. The engine was ticking over.

"Yes, everything's okay, Ted!" Leader answered.

Dawson poked his head out of the cabin window.

"I've got the dynamite, sir," he announced. "I suppose I act as bomber?"

"You and Jimmy," Rapson said. "It's going to be primitive, I'm afraid, but we've got to make the best of it. You two had better have these" he added, and handed over the elephant guns. "If those things can stop elephants, I reckon they ought to be good enough against a 'plane, always provided you can hit it, and the kick doesn't turn us over!"

He climbed up into the machine and settled himself into the pilot's seat, in front of the side-by-side seats into which Dawson and Leader sat a few moments later. He opened the throttle and presently threw off the brakes. The Moth leapt forward with a roar and tore down the stretch which had been hardly won from the jungle and was intended to be a landing-ground for the next few weeks, perhaps months, if work was held up by anything. Like a bird, the 'plane took off, cleared the surrounding jungle and then Rapson turned out of the slight wind and knew he was headed for the coast.

"Hundred odd miles to go," he muttered. "Won't take us long, though!"

For a while he followed the railway, but as that did not go in a straight course, owing to mountains which it had been decided to by-pass—some day, perhaps, new towns would spring up on the route—he presently had only his instruments to guide him, until once more he saw the line beneath him.

He glanced over his shoulder and saw Leader and Dawson calmly fixing detonators to sticks of dynamite. His face was set grimly when he turned away. He was very worried about everything: he was flying to obey orders, and those orders implied, even if they had not been explicit on the point, that he was to intervene on the Government side. It meant killing men, and Ted Rapson disliked the whole idea even although those men were rebels. He was a surveyor, not a soldier. His work in life was not warlike: it was concerned with helping to build railways which were designed to open new fields to man's endeavour and pleasure.

"Almost inclined to disobey Darcy's orders!" he gritted; but was given no chance to do so. Afar off, he had seen the roofs of Monrovia, the seaport and capital which was set on the comparatively narrow stretch of low coast-land, back of which the mountains reared. There was smoke above the roofs —and coming towards him, Ted Rapson saw an aeroplane.

Rapson gazed at it through his glasses. It was a red-winged, red-bodied, low-wing monoplane. It looked exactly like a bird, because there was no sign of wheels. Obviously the machine had a retractable undercarriage, and Rapson knew that it was a Heinkel.

"German make!" he murmured, as, realising that the Heinkel was climbing, he set the Moth to do like-wise. He had read enough about air fighting to know that the advantage lay with the fighter who could obtain height over his opponent. Moreover, Ted Rapson had served in the R.A.F. on short service, regarding it as a valuable part of his training in aerial surveying. He would have had few qualms about joining issue with a fighting 'plane—if only he had a machine-gun mounted. He wondered had the Heinkel one? If it belonged to Kebreau, it certainly would

B

have, since the would-be ruler of Liberia was unlikely
to buy or in some other way acquire an unarmed
'plane to help him in his revolt.

Dawson tapped Rapson on the shoulder and pointed
a hand towards the climbing red-winged machine.
Ted nodded, turned, and saw that his two companions
had left off the job of seeing to the dynamite and had
their elephant guns in hand. They had slid back the
panels of the cabin.

Ted realised that the Heinkel was climbing faster
than the Moth. He did his utmost to counter this,
but found he could not. He flattened out and sent the
Moth roaring through the air with the throttle wide
open after banking and turning so that he was speeding
away from the Heinkel. With every ounce of power
thrusting the machine through the air, Rapson obtained top speed, and then at last pulled the nose up
at an angle considerably beyond normal climbing
angle. The result was to convert speed into climb—
and the danger was to overshoot, as it were. If he
did that, the exhausted 'plane would drop heavily
when it reached its peak, and go out of control, with
a consequent loss of the very height for which he had
carried out the manœuvre. But Ted Rapson had
flown the Moth too often not to be sensitive to its
every mood, and his whole body seemed to tell him
when to push the stick forward and so bring the machine
out of its climb safely.

When he did so, he saw, with a feeling of relief, that
he had actually succeeded in over-topping the Heinkel,
which had lost height at the beginning through coming
round to follow when the Moth suddenly changed

course. Rapson saw it battling again for height, but he believed he could fly over it before success came to it.

He looked back—signed to his companions, who nodded that they understood; and then the Moth roared madly across the sky, with the Heinkel on its right. From the Heinkel came spurting smoke, but not from its exhaust.

"A machine-gun!" grated Rapson, and then felt as if someone had let off a giant cracker right in his ear. It came a second or so after those smoke-puffs from the Heinkel, and Rapson knew that Dawson had let fly with his elephant gun. Smoke filled the cabin and Rapson seemed to bite it. Dawson fired his second barrel so quickly that Rapson scarcely realised the second shot. He had been watching the smoke spewing from the Heinkel—and knew that the machine was fitted with a synchronised machine-gun, which was the reason why the Heinkel, unable to gain height, was winging in with raised nose. It had to go into battle nose-forward—whereas Rapson realised that the Moth, although she had no machine-gun, could attack from either side. That was an advantage likely to weigh against the presence of the machine-gun on the Heinkel, and Rapson almost gyrated in the air to give Dawson and Leader every opportunity.

Bullets spewed from the Heinkel, heavy charges from the elephant guns. Rapson took the Moth right over the Heinkel, and a sidelong glance showed him Jimmy Leader, looking as if he were going to slide out of the machine as Rapson banked a little. But Leader did not slide out: he fired his big gun—and the gleaming cover of the cabin, domed out of the red body of the Heinkel, was smashed. And the Moth finished the turn into which Rapson had taken it while the Heinkel slid on to its tail and went into a spin.

"Gosh, Jimmy got him!" roared Ted, and then saw that the Heinkel was being brought back into control. Rapson hated the very thought of attacking a wounded foe, but this was war. . . . He brought the Moth about so that Dawson could get to bear on the Heinkel, but although the elephant gun roared, the red 'plane was still in the air, and bullets were spurting from its machine-gun.

"Tail for me!" Rapson gritted, and once more adopted that ruse of speeding away, only to zoom, come out of it in time, and to find himself right behind the Heinkel. The latter's machine-gunner-pilot was unable to do anything except try to manœuvre out of his dangerous position: but Dawson's gun blasted away the Heinkel's tail and the machine went sliding down towards the tree-tops.

Something shot out of it.

"Bailed out!" Rapson roared, as a pilot-parachute bellied in the air.

"Durn good thing he did!" came from Dawson, as the Heinkel met the trees and instantly burst into flames. "Though I'm thinking he'll maybe roast in the forest fire!"

Dry as tinder, the trees caught fire—and as the Moth climbed and went speeding towards distant Monrovia, enormous flames leapt into the air—and Rapson knew that there was the beginning of a fire which would destroy some of Liberia's valuable timber.

But Rapson's thoughts were fixed on Monrovia, over which a black pall of smoke had increased during the ten minutes of combat.

CHAPTER 11

REVOLT!

RAPSON flew over Monrovia to take stock of the situation. There was a vicious exchange of firing between occupants of the Executive Mansion and unseen men in surrounding houses. There were some isolated street battles in progress, and a number of buildings were in flames. One of them, Rapson realised, was that which housed offices of the construction company.

Back of the town, sky and distance were blotted out by the raging forest fire caused by the fallen aeroplane, and when Rapson went down to get a better view of the town, bullets were immediately humming about the machine.

"That," he grated, "means whoever's in command—Kebreau, of course—knew we had been appealed to. He sent out the Heinkel to stop us. The rebels have got machine-guns!" He yelled the last few words over his shoulder, as several machine-guns began firing from roof-tops.

Jimmy Leader did not answer Rapson. Instead, he replied to the machine-gun fire by flicking dynamite over the side. Risking being found by bullets, he leant out of the cockpit to see where his explosive fell, and was not at all surprised to see that it missed houses and dropped into the street.

"I'm no bomber, Ted!" he yelled. "But that'll let 'em know what we mean to try!"

He saw Rapson nod his head as the machine banked and turned. Ted sped across the town towards the tallest building near Government House. Hot fire was being poured into the latter.

"See what you can do here, both of you!" Rapson called back, and a few moments later, sticks of dynamite were pitched overboard. Dawson, thanks to war-flying experience, was able to act with some measure of judgment and told Leader when to throw. The result was satisfying to the extent that the dynamite fell nearer the building aimed at than had Leader's first sticks. Rapson came round and back, and the two "bombers" went into action again. Their explosives missed the building, but rebels lying behind barricades sprang to their feet and ran for better shelter: that is, those of them who were not blown to bits by the dynamite.

"It's going to be sheer luck if we hit the houses we aim at, Jim," Dawson said to his companion. To Rapson, through the telephone, he said: "Let's concentrate on the houses round the Mansion. If necessary, we can drop all we've got and go back for more."

"All right—let it all go!" Rapson agreed. "We've got to do something and keep at it, because our men won't be able to get in for hours!"

That was a disturbing fact which had been worrying him ever since he had seen a long stretch of the railway torn up twenty miles or so out of Monrovia. There was also the possibility that the line might have been mined farther out. If so, the workers from railhead would be in for trouble, indeed.

Rapson brought the 'plane round, nose once more towards the main centre of the fighting. Dawson and Leader began throwing out their dynamite, which went off in a series of explosions, sound of which was drowned by the roar of the engine, but their visible effects observable. Holes were torn in the streets, iron roofs of houses gouted up, fires were started; and from some of the houses men were seen running— while rifle and machine-gun fire spurted from the Executive Mansion and harried them as they fled.

The smoke which had been swirling up from the building when the 'plane arrived, had disappeared: and Rapson was able to see that the place looked as though it had been struck by heavy shells. He guessed, however, that it had been bombed by the Heinkel, which had then postponed further attack in order to go and meet the Moth. Houses round about were now on fire, owing to the work of the dynamiting airmen, who flung their last few sticks into a bunch of scurrying men. There was no doubt about these being rebels, because they had rushed out of a house from which bullets had been fired, and a number of hand bombs had been flung at the Government building.

"That's the lot, Ted!" Dawson exclaimed, and Rapson sent the 'plane hurtling across the town, dropping as if the intention was to fire at the fugitives. These were going in all directions and unseen marksmen fired at them from here and there.

Ted took the machine round and climbed. Ahead, everything was blotted out by an ever-increasing

volume of smoke: it was as if Monrovia were cut off
from the rest of Africa by an impenetrable wall of
black and grey, shot with red and orange where flames
leapt. Rapson realised that had there been an offshore
wind the inhabitants of Monrovia would have been
facing an enemy more implacable than at present: but
the wind was blowing from the sea and, bad as that
was, since it meant the forest fire would spread
disastrously, it at least meant the saving of
Monrovia.

But it also meant a hazardous, or at least unpleasant,
flight for those in the Moth. Rapson climbed ever
higher and higher before he dared to head inland. He
went out over the sea to gain the height necessary to
overtop the pall of smoke, and when at last he turned
and went tearing inland, it was to fly over what
looked like a vast storm-tossed sea. Presently, he was
able to pick out the railway line, saw the long gap in
it, and then the train that was bringing meagre help
to the loyalists in Monrovia. It was stationary.
Obviously, the men in it realised that it would be
impossible for it to pass through the inferno. They
could not, Rapson knew, be aware of the broken line,
nor of the cause of the forest fire, which had spread down
from the mountains on to the plain through which the
line ran.

"Better drop 'em a message!" Rapson told Leader.
"Tell about the gap—they'll know what they're up
against then."

Rapson circled above the train while Leader scrawled
a note on the side of one of the dynamite boxes. Then
the 'plane swooped down and seemed to skim just

over the earth as Leader dropped the message a little
to one side of the train. As Rapson climbed, he saw
several men leap out of a wagon, and knew that the
message had been seen. Then he was speeding north-
west again, with the wind-borne smoke following, as
though it would engulf the machine.

He set the 'plane down at railhead, and the work of
refuelling began at once. Dynamite was loaded, and
at last the machine set off on its second flight. As
they neared the coast Rapson saw that rivers and
swamps had served to keep the fire from spreading,
but it was still necessary to climb high. There was no
sign of the train where he had last seen it. Later, he
saw it a short distance from the torn-up rails. It was
empty.

"They had to go on," he said, "because the fire was
driving in on them. To proceed was less dangerous
than staying or even going back, because the flames
would follow after them, while ahead the fire would
have burnt itself nearly out. He was able, presently,
to pick out, when he flew low, tiny moving figures on the
permanent way, showing now and again through the
smoke when the wind dispersed it. The men were
plodding along, bent on getting into town. The
capital was visible to the airmen by now, and after
a while they were over it. Rebels who had returned
to the ruins of their former positions were seen scurrying for other cover—and Rapson realized that to bomb
them would be to imperil loyalists. But one building,
near the Government building on top of which the
Liberian flag was flying, was still occupied by men
firing at the defended edifice. It had escaped during

the first attack by the railway workers, who now concentrated on it, and plastered it with dynamite.

"Looks as if there's been an assault on the Mansion!" Rapson said. On the ground in front of it were huddled heaps that he knew were men, dead, dying men. Only one ship was in the harbour, and that had no flag at its masthead. As the 'plane circled and dynamite crashed on the attacked house, Rapson saw men hurrying on to this vessel, and others were skipping from cover to cover as they went through narrow streets—all, apparently, making for the docks. Other men were in their wake, firing at them. Rearguard actions were being fought, but it was impossible for the fliers to say which were rebels.

From the house being bombed, there emerged several men, and only a devoted little group on the roof, remained, calmly firing their machine-gun at the 'plane. The men who had come out did not, as Rapson thought they might, make an attack on the Government building: they scattered and ran in the direction of the harbour.

"I've got it!" Rapson roared. "Those are rebels going on board that ship. These others are making for it, too; and the machine-gunners are standing by to draw our fire. After the fugitives!"

He brought the 'plane round. Dynamite crashed and although it missed the house itself, shook it so that a wall toppled down in ruins. Rapson shoved after the fugitives, flying low. Screaming women and children, however, prevented any attempt to bomb the rebels, who now and then took pot-shots at the machine.

Along the coast large numbers of men were hurrying.

A few small boats, crowded with men, were pulling towards the lone ship in harbour.

"Bomb the ship, Ted!" It was Jim Leader who bellowed the suggestion, but Rapson shook his head.

"No!" he said. "We don't want to do any more killing than's necessary! By bombing the ship we'd simply turn the rebels back in desperation. By heaven, look!"

The fugitives along the coast had come to a halt, and were formed up, firing rapidly at a speeding lorry.

"That's why they were running away!" Rapson said. "I spotted the lorry come out of a street and had half a mind to go after it, in case they were rebels in it."

Dawson threw a couple of dynamite sticks over. They exploded a little in the rear of the rebels, some of whom were flung a distance by the concussion. The rest sprang to their feet and resumed their wild flight towards the harbour. The lorry charged after them, and there was an explosion amongst them.

"Those chaps have got bombs!" said Leader.

"Those chaps," came from Rapson, who had taken the machine low, and had been looking through his binoculars, "haven't got bombs. It's dynamite! They're our fellows!"

Even as he spoke, the lorry's bonnet was blown off by a shell fired by a light field-piece. A little while before that the gun had been flinging shells at the building from which the rebels had emerged when the 'plane attacked. Rapson and his companions had not seen the fight which had resulted in a bunch of rebels overcoming its crew. The men in the lorry were

flung out, some of them remaining where they fell.
The lorry was in flames. The survivors sprinted for
cover, but the fugitive rebels did not stay to join
issue. The field-piece bumped along the coast road—
until several sticks of dynamite exploded around it.
There was no direct hit: that was too much to hope
for. But the gun crashed into a deep hole caused by
the dynamite. Its crew, those of them who could,
scurried after their fellows, and Dawson and Leader
flung dynamite to speed them on their way.

From all over the town now men were streaming,
pursued by others, and whatever use the 'plane may
have been before, it was now of little help because of
the danger of killing loyalists; and in any case, all the
dynamite had been used up and there were only the
two elephant guns.

"Why the sudden turn of battle?" Rapson wondered. "Can't be solely because of us and that lorry-
load of workers!"

He flew over the Government building again.
Armed men were hurrying from it and going towards
the harbour. Others were entering neighbouring
houses, and machine-guns appeared on the roofs.
It was evident that while the rebels were being pursued, some of the loyalists were taking up strategic
positions against the possibility of a renewal of hostili-
ties. At a large number of points in the town, fighting
was still proceeding, but Rapson decided that the only
thing he could do was to keep on flying around for
the time being. He had seen that the small landing
ground just outside Monrovia was intact and he
would be able to make a landing, unless the battle was

resumed. Then he would have to get back to rail
head. He looked at his petrol gauge and knew he had
enough fuel if return was necessary.

"That ship's moving, Ted!" Jim Leader yelled the
information, and Rapson turned the machine towards
the harbour. The steamer was, indeed, leaving the
dockside. A large crowd of men were on the dock
obviously putting up a clamour. There were some
men swimming towards the moving vessel. A few
small boats, packed with men, were trying to reach it
Rapson realized what had made the ship start: a
couple of field-pieces were firing at it, and a large force
of loyalists, Frontier Force and Militia, was very near
the docks.

"Probably Kebreau's been killed!" said Rapson
"The rebels have therefore chucked up the job
Say, look!" His companions looked, and saw arm
being thrown to the ground as the loyalists approached
Hands went up, many of them waving handkerchief
in lieu of white flags.

"Looks like the end—except for a few dawn-shoot
ings," said Dawson, grimly. "Reckon we can go down
now, Ted?"

"I think so," Rapson agreed; and the machine went
racing over the town towards the landing-field. Out
side the town, Rapson understood the reason for the
sudden débâcle of the rebels: by ancient wagons
by cycle and car, crowds of people were hurrying
in. Evidently, they had been forced to leave
their villages by the forest fire. The rebels who
had doubtless hoped to bring off a swift coup and
seize the town, were not prepared to stand against a

frenzied mob of fugitives, many of them, no doubt, armed. But for the fire, these people from the villages would have known nothing of events until the *fait accompli* and they found themselves with a new Government, and, as so often is the way of things, they would have accepted it as something which they were unable to alter. Dynamiting by the 'plane had probably played its grim and effective party by demoralizing the rebels who had, no doubt, hoped that the Heinkel would prevent its coming.

"Might have, too!" Rapson thought, as he set the machine down. "What the deuce is that?" He pushed his head out of the cabin and poked his fingers into engine-deadened ears.

"Church bells, Ted!" Jimmy Leader got out of the machine. "Peals of victory, no less!"

"Which doesn't seem complete, yet," said Rapson as he got down. "There's still some fighting going on."

Muffled by the distance, the sound of firing came to them.

"And look!" Dawson stabbed the air with blackened hand. He pointed seawards. The steamer they had seen leaving the dock was pouring out vast clouds of black smoke, and the sea around it was erupting fountains of water. "The field-guns are trying to sink her, Ted!"

"Rather the Liberians did it than that we had bombed 'em," Rapson said, grimly. "After all, it's their fight, not ours, really. Wonder if Darcy's all right?"

"I'll try and get in to find out, Ted," Leader volunteered. "We'd be wise not to leave the machine, perhaps?"

"We're all staying by it!" was Rapson's decision. "We'll have been seen landing, and somebody'll come out soon. I'm not going to let either of you risk going in while guns are still popping! We'll refuel from our stores while we're waiting. Here's the key!"

CHAPTER III

UNDERCURRENTS

THEY were still at the refuelling job when a lorry, packed with armed men, came roaring towards the ground.

"In you get!" rapped Ted, and flung away the emptied drum. He was about to screw up the petrol tank when Leader, who had examined the approaching lorry through his glasses, said:

"Okay, Ted! It's Government, judging by the flag it's flying!"

"Well, stand to with those guns!" Rapson said. "I'll have the engine going in case!"

Precautions, however, were unnecessary. The lorry rattled to a standstill, and two men jumped down.

"There's Darcy!" Rapson said, relief in his voice. He walked to meet George Darcy, the man in charge of the administrative side of the contract and part of whose work it was to keep the Liberian authorities sweet. There had been keen competition to secure the Concession and from what Darcy had learnt afterwards, not a little bribery and political wire-pulling on the part of some of the firms who tendered. It was partly the revelation of this which had caused the reorganization of civil service posts that had resulted in Kebreau's being dismissed. While Kebreau had been in office, Darcy had been subjected to all

manner of annoyance and all kinds of obstructions—
designed, as he knew, to retard work. There was a
time limit, with heavy penalties attached, to the
contract; and Kebreau, who had been Finance
Minister, no doubt reckoned on getting a rake-off
in the event of the penalties being enforced.

It was therefore a relief to Darcy in particular
and all those engaged on the job, when Kebreau
had been dismissed. Nobody had imagined that he
would break out in another place!

"God! But I'm glad to see you, Rapson!" Darcy
gripped Ted's hand when they met.

"Mighty glad to see you," Rapson smiled, grimly.
He looked at the Liberian officer with Darcy. "Pleased
to see you, too, Captain Jefferson."

The Captain nodded somewhat abruptly, and
Rapson caught a queer look in Darcy's eyes.

"The President wishes to see you, Mr. Rapson,"
Jefferson said. "I'll leave a guard over your machine,
of course."

"Thanks!" Rapson looked as if, failing that promise,
he would have refused to leave the 'plane. "Are
my friends wanted, too?"

"No—only you," was the answer, and Jefferson
snapped out a command, which brought half-a-dozen
of his men from the lorry. They went over to the
'plane with Darcy, who was going to shake hands with
Leader and Dawson. Walking beside Rapson, he
said:

"Don't get riled, Ted! But the President is in a
bit of a fume because you didn't blast that steamer!
Say, don't think he's ungrateful for what you did, but

he thinks you should have tried to stop that crowd of rebels from getting away."

"I can tell him why," Rapson said, with a mirthless chuckle. "What about Jameson and the other fellows in the office?"

"Jameson was—was killed," Darcy said. "But I'll explain while we're on the way in. Well, you two!" he shook hands warmly with Leader and Dawson. "All correct? No wounds?"

Dawson grinned and pushed up his left sleeve. Rapson had not known about it, but Dawson showed a handkerchief bound tightly about his biceps.

"Got a bullet through the flesh there," he said. "Nothing much to worry about. Pretty clean wound and Jimmy here sucked it almost dry for me!"

"You'd better come with us and have it properly dressed," Rapson said quickly. "I've got to go and see the President."

"Perhaps I will," Dawson agreed. "Jimmy can finish refuelling and oiling, can't you?" he glanced at his companion, who nodded.

"These soldiers are staying on guard," Rapson told Leader. "The fighting isn't all over yet, as you can hear."

"A little street fighting that's all," came from Jefferson, who had arrived at the machine. "If you're ready, gentlemen?"

They were. They went back to the lorry, climbed into it. Darcy got Rapson and Dawson in the rear, one on each side of him, and they squatted on the floor. Armed men were at the sides, ready to fire if anybody even looked suspiciously at them!

"Well, what about it, sir?" Rapson asked, when the lorry was rattling towards Monrovia. "All I got from Leader was that Jameson telegraphed to ask us to come in and was cut off. He did say something about Kebreau, though."

"Yes, it was Kebreau all right," Darcy admitted. "Everything started so suddenly that the Government was taken off guard. I was with the President when firing broke out. I can tell you now that Kebreau's men were landed from the steamer during the night, fully equipped. They were in Frontier Force uniform, or something very like it so that they could move about without being suspected. I——" He stopped, as the lorry bumped into a hole, almost capsized, but presently was rattling on again.

"Well, as I was saying, I was with the President," Darcy resumed. "One or two prisoners were taken and brought in. They told us about Kebreau and just then an aeroplane came over and began to bomb the building. The President asked if I could get in touch with you and ask you to come in the Moth. I asked him whether he thought we used bombs for railroad building. He almost barked that dynamite was used! Wanted as many men as we'd arms for to come down, too. I had to agree, Ted! He sent some men out—at risk of their lives, to get to the offices and give orders to Jameson. He's dead!"

"So you said," Rapson murmured.

"Found out on the way to the landing-field," Darcy said. "We stopped at the offices, or what's left of 'em. They've been shelled almost to blazes. Tester was there—he died in my arms." He gulped a little. "He

said a shell crashed through the office while Jameson
was telegraphing you. Took his head clean off, poor
chap, and Tester got his from a flying splinter. In
the chest. I heard him groaning amongst the wreckage,
Rapson!"

"Poor devil!" murmured Ted. "I say, Mr. Darcy,
if Jameson hadn't said that it was by your orders, I
would not have butted in on this game. Why on earth
should we, after all, eh? It's a dangerous thing to
interfere in politics."

"I know," Darcy admitted. "I told the President
I wasn't inclined to do anything. He told me that if
Kebreau won I could expect a tricky cancellation of
the concession. It seemed to me I'd better do what the
President asked."

"H'm," grunted Rapson. "Kebreau may have got
it in the neck to-day, but there's always to-morrow.
If he has another shot and wins, we'd be finished for
certain. However, you're the boss!"

The drive through Monrovia did not take long.
Despite being engaged in conversation, Rapson had
been able to observe conditions on the way. Buildings
were wrecked, some were still burning. Men and women
and children were scratching amongst the debris, some
of them, doubtless, seeking personal belongings, others,
no doubt, snatching at the chance of loot. Stretcher
parties were at work, removing dead and wounded.
Some of the scenes were distinctly unpleasant: Ted
supposed that they were inevitable in the circumstances. In civil wars the passions of men are let
loose: personal hatreds flare up with the opportunity
for vengeance. Rapson was glad when the strong

guard outside the Government building allowed him and Darcy to enter.

President Adams Coolidge received them in a room whose windows were smashed. A shell had passed right through the room and smashed a great hole in a far wall. Mr. Coolidge was a six-foot Negro of not unpleasing appearance. He was dressed in a black frock coat and striped trousers. The high, starched collar above the putty-coloured waistcoat looked very uncomfortable, but the President did not seem to feel any discomfort. His dark eyes glinted behind heavy-rimmed spectacles, and when he smiled, two gold teeth gleamed amongst his own surprisingly white ones.

"Thank you in the name of the Republic, Mr. Rapson!" When he spoke his voice was cultured, and to anybody unfamiliar with the history of the Black Republic, which had been formed to provide a home for freed American slaves and their descendants, would have sounded incongruous.

Rapson bowed slightly. Mr. Coolidge's manner did not suggest that he wanted to make a complaint, and when a servant had brought in whisky and soda, he raised his glass in salutation, still very affable. The tinkling ice in the glass was like music to Rapson after the recent horror, and he downed the drink gratefully.

"Had you run out of dynamite, Mr. Rapson?" President Coolidge asked the question suddenly, but smoothly. Ted made no attempt to hide the fact that he knew why the President had sent for him, nor to take the advantage the question had given him: he knew very well that if he said he had exhausted his supply of dynamite the statement could be easily disproved.

"No, sir," he answered. "I had a few sticks left."

"Then why didn't you atack that steamer?" The President was still very suave, and Ted wondered what was behind all this. "It's not unlikely that you could have prevented it sailing."

"That's precisely why I followed the course I did, sir," Rapson said. "I thought that by allowing at least those rebels who were boarding the ship to get away, I should to that extent make a recovery impossible. Also, I should be saving lives."

"Lives of rebels!" The President was crisp and harsh now. "Lives of men who, if they got into power, would take away the liberty of the people! Having got away, they are a potential danger to Liberia."

"I'm neither a soldier nor a Liberian, sir," Rapson reminded him, calmly. President Coolidge smiled and swung his body to and fro from the waist up, as if a nod of the head would not be sufficient to express his acceptance of Rapson's assertion.

"I want to put the position plainly to both of you," he waved a hand which took in Darcy. "I do not know yet whether Kebreau is alive, but even if he is dead, the basic fact of the situation would remain the same. We took one of his lieutenants prisoner and while the fighting was in progress we—er—questioned him."

Darcy gave Rapson a swift glance, as if to intimate that to be "questioned" in such circumstances was not likely to be a pleasant ordeal.

"The prisoner informed us," Mr. Coolidge went on, "that Kebreau is now merely a pawn in the hands of a foreign Power. That aeroplane you brought down, Mr. Rapson, was of foreign make." Ted nodded, but said nothing, as the President continued: "That and all the arms were supplied by foreign agents. The steamer which took away those rebels landed them down the coast. There was a second aeroplane, but it met with an accident before the time for the rising. The ship sailed with false papers, and came into Monrovia after discharging her munitions and a number of Europeans who, for face-saving purposes, are supposed to be foreign volunteers."

"It was done in Spain!" Darcy spoke quickly. "But there it was not a case of a couple of 'planes and a meagre supply of arms!"

"The reason for small measures here," said Mr. Coolidge, "is surely plain? Liberia is not an armed country. Its policy has always been a peaceful one. We Liberians, although we joined the League of Nations, have hitherto had but a small place in international affairs. But if Kebreau had succeeded to-day, you can depend on it—the prisoner admitted so much —that he would have 'invited' and been given financial assistance under 'guarantees'. Those guarantees were to take the form of a large foreign legion, and economic and other concessions."

"Then why didn't Kebreau get sufficient support at the start?" Rapson asked.

"He was supposed to have had more," the President answered. "A second ship with men and munitions foundered. Kebreau could not put things off because the rebels in Monrovia had been warned that to-day was the day. They'd been warned several times before,

but for unknown reasons, the day had been postponed. It caused discontent, and Kebreau did not
want to risk adding to it. So he decided to strike,
hoping for surprise to give him success. So that no
suspicion should be created before the actual rising,
the telegraph wires were not cut, although the railway
line was torn up some distance out of town. Kebreau
had somebody tapping the telegraph, which is how he
learnt that you were asked to come in. That's why
he sent the Heinkel out."

"All very interesting, sir," Rapson agreed. "But
what could the—er—foreign Power hope to gain by
fostering rebellion here and, as I suppose was intended,
seeing that their own form of government was set
up?"

"Unfortunately," Mr. Coolidge said, "Liberia is
sadly undeveloped. But there are many kinds of
minerals, as you probably know. It's to develop our
mineral resources that you are building the railway;
the first of several, we hope. Gold and tin, and copper
and zinc—especially copper—are more valuable to-
day than they have ever been. For any country to
obtain what may be called a controlling interest in
Liberia, therefore, would be of great importance.
But that is not all."

He indicated the whisky and soda, and conversation
flagged for a few moments. Then he resumed, speaking
now with what it was obvious he intended to be real
gravity.

"Events in Europe," he said, "have created many
changes which affect Britain." He paused to watch,
it seemed to Rapson, the effect of his words. Darcy

frowned. Ted himself toyed with his glass and let the ice ring against it. "The Mediterranean route to the East," Mr. Coolidge went on, "is not now as safe as it used to be. There's been talk about, in the event of war, the British Navy and Mercantile Marine making use perforce of the West Coast of Africa route. Certain Powers would be in a strong position if they had submarine and air bases at their disposal in friendly countries. You understand?"

Rapson had met President Coolidge before, so it was not a surprise to him to hear the Negro dilate on international affairs in this way. The brief statement had a great deal of wisdom packed into it, whether it was the result of the "questioning" of the prisoner or a theory worked out by the President.

"Yes, sir, I think I understand," Rapson said. "It seems to me that, as a member of the League of Nations, Liberia should put its case before that body."

President Coolidge smiled mirthlessly.

"A protest made by the League," he said, "would meet with the fate of protests made regarding Spain, for instance. It would be denied that any official foreign support had been given to Kebreau. Even if we got the prisoner, and others like him, to sign statements, what good would that do? None whatever! Until the right moment arrives—and even if Kebrèau had succeeded, it is impossible to say that this would have been regarded by other nations as the right moment—until it does arrive, gentlemen, Liberia has got to stand on her own feet. Warned by what has happened, the Government will take all steps to prepare against any further trouble. I need not suggest what those steps will be. Not in full, at least. But I want to mention something which concerns you and your work."

Rapson realized that the President had reached the point at which he had been aiming all through the conversation. He waited for Mr. Coolidge to proceed.

"If Kebreau had succeeded," the President said, "he was going to cancel your concession and stop work on the railway, because, designed as it is to end at the frontier between Liberia and Sierre Leone, it will provide a route which, in the event of war—and the circumstances here that I suggested a few moments ago—it would be valuable for the movement of British troops, dispatched to attack enemy bases from the rear."

"Mr. Kebreau——" Rapson began, but Coolidge interrupted to say:

"He calls himself General now—General Kebreau, whose aim is, as he puts it, to free the Liberian people from a Constitution which is crippling the country, and to set up what he calls a Liberian National-Socialist State."

"I don't care what he's aiming at," said Rapson. "He seems to be a particularly low blackguard. He got fired for corrupt practices and then had the audacity to pose as a patriot! In his own new State I imagine he'd have been liquidated, instead of being merely sacked. Yes, sir, I see how his success would have affected us."

"I'm glad you do," said the President. He looked at Darcy, as if wanting to hear his opinion. Mr. Darcy gave it.

"Judged by what has happened in other totalitarian states, we'd be just about mud if Kebreau came into power, sir!"

"Exactly!" said the President, smoothly. "I am under no illusions about Kebreau. I don't believe he will accept to-day's defeat. He'll try again. I am going to call the Government and put forward a scheme for recruiting a foreign legion. I'd like to meet my ministers and be able to say that certain European workers on the railway are willing to join the legion. What do you think, gentlemen?"

CHAPTER IV

TRAITOR IN CAMP

TED RAPSON looked at President Coolidge and laughed.

"You worked up a very good case there, sir," he said. "Are there any penalties to refusal?"

"What Rapson means," put in Darcy, "is, are you putting any pressure on us and our men to join your foreign legion?"

"No pressure whatever!" President Coolidge spoke with a ring of sincerity in his voice. "Nor do I stipulate anything more than that the railway workers in the legion shall defend the line if it is attacked. Actually, you would become a defence force, with authority from the Government. At present, you are just workers in a foreign land, dependent for protection upon what help we can give you. I'd like to know that you accepted authority to defend the line—and when the job's done, you'd be free from the Service."

"I understand, sir," Darcy said. "You want us to go back and hear what the men have to say on the matter? What about the Liberians with us, and the natives?"

"We'll deal with them, Mr. Darcy," was the answer. "I'm glad you've seen the matter in the right light. I take it that you do, too, Mr. Rapson?"

"If anybody comes up and tries monkey tricks with my job," Ted Rapson said, grimly, "he'll have to reckon with me, whether I'm in a legion or not! But I see that your plan regularizes things, so I'm agreeable."

"Excellent!" President Coolidge almost purred the word. "I regret that several of your men were killed or wounded when their lorry was shelled. You can leave the injured down here and we'll do our very best for them. They're already in hospital."

"I'd like to see them," Darcy said, and the President summoned an officer and gave instructions for Darcy and Rapson to be taken to the hospital. It seemed that orders had already been given for the survivors of the lorry-load of men to go to the flying-ground, and after visiting the hospital and sympathizing with the wounded, the two hurried back to the field.

Captain Jefferson was with them, so that he could take back to the President the decision of the men when Darcy put the foreign legion plan up to them. It was considered that the answers of these men would be an index to those of the whites who had had to stay at railhead. Coolidge's idea was that if he could put forward his plan together with a substantial backing, he would have no difficulty in getting his ministers to agree. Then he intended to appeal to all "safe" foreigners in Liberia. He felt that the existence of a foreign legion, made up in part, perhaps, of men who had served in other armies, would lend stiffening to his own inexperienced forces.

Rapson left it to Darcy, naturally, to approach the men. Dawson and Jim Leader immediately signified agreement, and a number of others followed their example. One or two protested that they had signed on to work, and not to fight. Darcy explained that they were not only free to refuse but would not suffer as a result. In the end, the whole bunch agreed, and Darcy scribbled a note to the President and gave it to Captain Jefferson.

"I'll send down news of what happens at railhead," Darcy promised. "I'm going up to see the men. Mind if I have your seat in the 'plane, Leader?"

"Not at all," was the answer, and Darcy gave orders for some of the men to stay where the line had been torn up, and set to work repairing it with the help of labourers who would be sent down by train. There was also work to be done on telegraph-line repairs, but this could be left to the authorities in Monrovia.

"There's only one thing we ought to do, Rapson," said Darcy. "We ought to go and see the British Consul here and tell him what we've agreed to do."

"I don't think so," Rapson demurred. "You see, Darcy, we're acting on our own. It would be unwise to notify British authorities. If the President cares to pass the information on, that's his look-out. Actually, we're just a volunteer defence force, pledging ourselves to tackle anybody who tries to interfere with us and our work. In any case, I'd suggest leaving things as they are for the present."

After some argument, Darcy agreed to Rapson's suggestion and presently was seated beside Dawson, behind Ted, in the 'plane. It took off easily, and climbed high, so that it would not be necessary to fly through the smother of smoke which still hung over the hills.

At railhead, Darcy lost no time in calling a meeting of the whites, other than certain men who were informed that they were to go into Monrovia with the train that was taking down material for the repair of the broken line.

"It's not my doing," he told them. "The Government has all the say. But I can tell you that there were several of your countrymen found dead or wounded after the fighting."

The half-dozen men accepted the situation phlegmatically, and in due course left railhead. In the meantime, Darcy addressed the other whites, put the President's plan before them, and left it to each man to make his own decision. To Darcy's surprise, every man assured him he was willing to join the proposed legion. Darcy, therefore, was able to send this information down when, in due time, the train left railhead.

President Coolidge acted with dispatch. He sent Captain Jefferson up, so that all the men could take the oath in proper form. With Jefferson were other Liberian officers who held meetings of the labourers, worked themselves and their audiences into a frenzy and in the end had well-nigh every man enlisted. This was not merely for railway defence, but for general service in the event of another rising.

This campaigning went on for several days and somewhat interfered with the work on the line. When it was finished, Darcy, still at railhead, found that arrangements had been made for Liberian Frontier Force officers to stay there to train the men in the use of arms. Machine-guns were sent up—and Ted Rapson, with an eye to eventualities, had one fitted to the aeroplane. Stocks of rifles and ammunition were also brought up, and railhead was by turns ringing to the clang of hammers, the screech of cranes, and all the noise of railway work, and the barking of sergeants drilling recruits.

The telegraph had long since been repaired and word came up from Monrovia that no sign had been found of Kebreau. A number of his officers, taken prisoners, had been tried and sent to prison: the Liberian Government did not have recourse to the death sentence—yet. Nothing had been heard of the escaped steamer since it left Monrovia, where life had settled down almost to normalcy, except that men were drilling hard, and, doubtless, the Government had its secret agents working in the hope of uncovering information of any further projected rebellion.

As the weeks went by without disturbance, the line was pushed ahead. Gangs of natives were clearing a way through the jungle. Sleepers were being put down and rails laid. Cuttings were being blasted through low hills. The iron road of civilization was pushing its way forward, and peace reigned in Liberia.

Darcy arrived at railhead one day with news that was not altogether welcomed by Rapson.

"The President is coming up, Ted," Darcy said. "He's going to kill two birds with one stone, as it were. He'll inspect what he likes to call 'the railroad defence army', and also the work going on at the bridge over the river. It's supposed to be a surprise visit. In any case, the 'troops' aren't to know. Coolidge wants to see how quickly they can be turned out, he says!"

"Confound him!" growled Rapson. "It means the work'll be delayed. When's he coming?"

D

"Three days' time," was the answer. "How about the bridge?"

"By then," said Rapson, "we shall have the middle pier finished, and be ready to throw out the span to it."

"Fine!" Darcy exclaimed. "Will you be able to let him see the span being put in position?"

"If things go according to schedule, yes," Rapson promised. "I suppose you'll come up with him? Good!" he grinned when Darcy replied. "That'll mean I shall be able to carry on with the job. I hate inspection parties. What happens first—inspection of the bridge or the 'troops'?"

"Bridge," was the answer. "I got the President to agree to that so that the work should not be interrupted. The 'troops' turn out after the work's over."

After looking round the job at railhead, Darcy returned to Monrovia. Because he wished to have the centre pier in position, Rapson confided to some of his colleagues and asked them to keep their men hard at it during the next two days. The result was an orderly hustle, in which good progress was made with the bridge; and when, at about midday, the train chugged to a standstill a short distance from railhead, and President Coolidge disembarked, Rapson had the satisfaction to knowing everything was set for a demonstration.

Accompanied by one of two officers, President Coolidge was escorted to the offices by Mr. Darcy, shown round numerous places where plate-laying was in progress, and then taken to the river.

"Where's Mr. Rapson?" he asked Darcy, who pointed to a tiny figure on a crane platform near the present extreme of the bridge.

"He's checking upon a survey line to the other side, sir," Darcy answered, having been told by Dawson that this had been rendered necessary by a report of one of the engineers. "That span which is being transported towards the middle of the river will be lowered into position presently, sir."

"I'd like to be close up when it's being done," the President suggested: and since he was the President and there was no reason why he should not have a close-up view, he was escorted on to the uncompleted bridge.

Ted Rapson, who had just completed his little job and found out that the reporting engineer was wrong, straightened up from his theodolite and told his native boy to pack it in its case. He looked back across the river and grinned at sight of the approaching company.

"No swearing, Johnson," he said to the craneman, who was waiting until the great span down below was ready for him to hoist by the dangling steel, hooked cable. "No swearing, and if you get rid of your baccy, you won't have to spit! This is His Excellency the President coming to see how bridges are built!"

"Strewth!" Johnson ejected his quid and mopped his brow. "Frock-coat and top-hat up here! My Gawd!"

"Dignity!" said Rapson solemnly. "If you only knew it, Johnson, nearly every Liberian who sees that top-hat and frock-coat, regards them as the symbol of what he can become! Theoretically, every

Liberian carries the Presidential top-hat and frock-coat in his grub-sack! Well, here they come!"

The Presidential party walked along the uncompleted bridge, stopping every now and then for Mr. Coolidge to look at something which interested him. Far below, the muddy river flowed lazily, oilily, and Ted Rapson knew that beneath its surface lurked crocodiles, cunning, patient brutes, waiting for a meal that had not to be hunted. Several men had lost their lives through a misstep, a fall into the water, followed by a scurrying of the hungry crocodiles and the death-scream of the doomed.

"Lower away, there!" The hail came from the men below the crane, and Johnson looked below to assure himself that all was ready. As he ran the hooked cable out, Ted Rapson yelled at him:

"Haul up, Johnson, haul up, for God's sake!"

He imagined his voice must be drowned by the tumult which had set in as President Coolidge shot off the end of the uncompleted bridge into the crocodile-infested river. Ted had seen it happen—seen, even while he was speaking to Johnson, a riveter get clumsily to his feet and stumble into the President.

"What——" Johnson half turned to look at Rapson, but the latter bellowed at him again to haul up the cable, adding:

"I'm going down by it. Snap to it, Johnson, for heaven's sake!"

Already, he could see crocodiles sweeping up the river towards the struggling President, whose top-hat was floating down river. A number of men were

streaking towards a boat on the bank, but Ted realized
that it was impossible for it to be pushed into the
river and reach the President in time to be of any
service to him. Grim-faced, Rapson waited while
the cable was rattling over the drum. The crane-arm,
which had been almost vertical, swung down a little,
and then the great hook at the end of the cable end
dangled before Ted. As the arm was eased in by
Johnson, bringing the hook near to him, he grabbed
at it, put a foot into the hook, clutched the cable
above him and snapped out the word "Go!"

"Okay, sir!" yelled Johnson. The crane-arm swept
over and downwards as the steel cable roared through
the pulley, and Rapson went stone-like through the
air. As in a blur he saw the scene beneath him: the
swimming President, splashing wildly, and the slither-
ing crocodiles pursuing him, the boat, launched now,
being rowed madly towards the centre of the river.
Then, suddenly, Ted struck the water not far from
where the President was, for Johnson had swung the
crane round to achieve this result. The black ruler
of the Black Republic swept towards Ted. With one
foot in the hook, and clutching the cable with one
hand, Rapson made a grab at Coolidge, caught him,
and yelled like fury to Johnson to haul up.

Rapson had the President by the collar of his
frock-coat and was praying that the stuff would not
give way as he felt himself yanked up from the water,
holding his man much as a puppy is held by his master.
As President Coolidge's feet left the water an ugly
brute of a crocodile, which had simply shot through
the last twenty yards, reached the spot. Ted saw the

monstrous jaws open, and with a swing which almost wrenched his arm from its socket, he sent the President sidewise. The cable whipped them both higher and the crocodile's jaw snapped to—empty.

A few moments later, Ted and the President were on the platform of Johnson's crane. Before Mr. Coolidge could say more than "Thank you!" Rapson was gone, pressing past men hurrying along the bridge. From the bank others, who had run to get rifles, were firing at the crocodiles, but Rapson was not interested in anybody—except one man.

He went in and out amongst the tangle of steel which hung over the river, asking a question here and there of workmen.

"Where's Lingard?" was the question, and he had to shout, because work had been resumed: the bridge could not wait for anything. The clang of hammers on rivets sounded musically, and it was at a bunch of riveters that Rapson presently stopped.

"Lingard!" he snapped, and a man looked up at him.

"Yes, sir?" Alf Lingard asked, gripping his riveter's gun. He was a black-haired man, with eyebrows which met above the bridge of his nose. His teeth were rather like discoloured fangs. His body, naked to the waist, was almost as dark as any Negro's.

"Hand over to someone and come with me!" said Ted. Lingard got to his feet. Rapson nodded to him to get on ahead: he felt safer with the man in front of him, for it was Alf Lingard whom he had seen get up and send President Coolidge tumbling off the bridge.

He took the man to the office, where Jim Leader was at work.

"What's wrong, Ted?" Leader asked. "There seems to have been hell to pay over at the bridge, judging by the row!"

Briefly, Rapson explained, and while he was doing so, the President and Mr. Darcy entered the office. After finding Lingard, Rapson had sent a messenger back to ask the President to come in. Mr. Coolidge was drenched to the skin: his frock-coat was clinging to him, his putty-coloured waistcoat was slimy, and his stiff collar was now a crumpled rag.

"I've asked for some clean dungarees to be brought for you, sir," Rapson told him, as he entered the office. "Here, by the way, is the man who caused you to drop into the river."

"It is forgiven," the President smiled. "Accidents will happen!"

"Accident be blowed!" Rapson exploded, forgetting the dignity of his guest. "I was looking—and that was the only accident about the whole thing! There wasn't any reason for Lingard to get up at that moment, I'm sure. As a matter of fact, he should have been holding down the rivet his mate below was ramming home. Have you seen him before, sir?"

"You're a darned liar!" came from Lingard, before President Coolidge could answer Ted's question. He stepped up as if he meant to drive his big fist into Ted's face, but Jimmy Leader sprang between them. President Coolidge looked at Lingard, then told Rapson that he did not remember having seen him before.

Suddenly, Ted switched to another matter, seemingly casually.

"Have you heard anything of Kebreau lately, sir?" he asked, and Lingard gave a little start. "It's all right, sir," Rapson added, grimly. "I asked the question for a particular reason." He snapped at Lingard then: "You're a rotten conspirator! You haven't learnt to control your eyes! Where's Kebreau? How much did he pay you for this stunt? Where did you meet him, and——"

Once more Lingard looked as if he would hurl himself at Ted, but again Jimmy Leader clamped a hand on his shoulder and swung him aside. Before Lingard could say anything in answer to Ted's rasped questions, the President, surprisingly, said:

"Tchck! Why trouble? I think it was an accident! As for Kebreau—poof! I don't care that for him!" He snapped his fingers. "Let this fellow go!"—and he winked at Rapson.

For a moment, Ted hesitated. Then he swung round on Lingard.

"Get out!" he snapped. "But—watch your step!"

"You go to hell!" came from Lingard, who turned on his heels and flung himself out of the office.

"Jimmy, pay him what's due and——" Rapson began, but Mr. Coolidge, the moment the door slammed behind Lingard, said, hastily:

"No, he is not to be dismissed, Mr. Rapson!" His voice was harsh now. No longer was he the man who had accepted as an accident the event which nearly cost him his life. No longer was he the man willing to allow the suspected workman to go free.

Yet he did not ask Rapson to call back Lingard. What he said was: "I think perhaps you're right about him, Mr. Rapson! I saw him once in Monrovia, months before the revolt. He was with Kebreau! But I did not reveal the fact when you asked me if I had seen him before."

Ted Rapson looked puzzled.

"Why not, sir?" he demanded. "If Lingard has been mixed up in the past with Kebreau, it's certain in my mind now that he did deliberately knock you off the bridge!"

"Undoubtedly," Mr. Coolidge agreed. "That man must know where Kebreau is! At least, I imagine so, and he should, if given his head, perhaps lead you to Kebreau!"

"Lead—me?" Ted jerked. "I'm a surveyor, not a secret service man, sir!"

"You forget, perhaps," said the President, "that you are a foreign legionary."

Rapson laughed. "No, sir, I haven't forgotten. I understand your meaning and I remember what you told us about Kebreau's intentions regarding the railway. I'll see that tabs are kept on Lingard's movements."

"Thank you," the President said. "Perhaps you won't mind my saying that it's a little perturbing to find one of your men a traitor. There may be others, too!"

Mr. Darcy, flustered, confused, and angry, seemed to have difficulty in breathing. "The trouble is," he said, "we can do nothing in the matter, except keep our eyes and ears open. The next thing to expect, probably, is sabotage. Does this mean," he appealed to the President, "that Kebreau is beginning a new campaign?"

"Probably," was the answer. "With assassination playing its part." He broke off as a knock sounded on the door. A workman entered, carrying the dungarees he had been sent for. Mr. Coolidge, with a broad grin, accepted them, and went into another room to make his change. When he came back he looked more like one of the railroad workers than a President, but by the time set for the inspection of the defence troops, he was once more in his frock-coat and striped trousers, although the top-hat was absent: a crocodile had gulped it down.

CHAPTER V

AIR "MAIL"

FOLLOWING the failure of what Rapson was certain had been a deliberate attempt to kill President Coolidge, constant watch was kept on Alf Lingard and the men with whom he was particularly friendly. A point which had worried Rapson, namely, how Lingard had received instruction, was cleared up, or at any rate, was explainable, by the discovery that Lingard had been one of a party of men who had gone down to Monrovia for a week-end break. Such breaks were part of routine, for life in camp was hard, and the men needed a change now and then. Lingard's visit to town had been at the week-end preceding the President's arrival in camp.

Rapson was perturbed, because the chances were long that Lingard would be in a position to bring off an attempt such as was staged. Rapson therefore argued that it was more than likely that other men were involved. If one did not get an opportunity, another might. By adopting the method of staging an "accident", instead of open attempts at assassination, Kebreau no doubt intended to achieve the removal of the President without anybody being able to accuse him of political murder. Failure, however, might force his hand, especially if he should have been able to bring his organization up to the point where action was possible, as well as necessary in order to strike before there could be any leakage regarding his plans.

If this were so, an attack might be made on the railway; it was common knowledge in Monrovia that the workers had been enlisted in a defence force. Intact, the railway would make it possible for that force to be hurried down to Monrovia if an outbreak occurred. Rapson had asked for frequent patrols to be sent out from the coast, while the defence force worked from railhead and the intermediate stations on the new iron road.

Work proceeded. The bridge was completed, and added a new responsibility. If it were destroyed while a train were on the far side, the workers at the new railhead there would be cut off. There were only a few boats available, and a very small number of rebels would be able to prevent the crossing of the river.

Occasionally, Rapson flew down to new offices in Monrovia for consultations with Darcy on matters concerning the work. Now and again he was out in the 'plane on surveying work beyond the limits yet reached; and as the weeks passed, and nothing happened, once again he, with everyone else, came to the conclusion that Kebreau—whose whereabouts were still unknown—was either not ready or had given up his idea of revolt.

Lingard, by either word or deed, had given no indication which would confirm Rapson's suspicion, and the President's belief, that he was in league with Kebreau. Richardson, one of the engine drivers, and Vic Blakey, an assistant engineer, were two of Lingard's little circle of friends. If they were fellow-conspirators, they gave no sign thereof. They were good workmen. Rapson, unostentatiously, arranged for Fareham, a man he could trust, to be Richardson's fireman, with instructions to watch the driver at all times. Fareham's reports gave no cause for alarm: Richardson's conduct was never out of the usual run.

Nevertheless, Ted Rapson had a foreboding.

"Can't explain it quite, Dave," he told Dawson, one evening, as they sat on the verandah of the temporary offices-cum-sleeping quarters which he and one or two officials occupied. "But I've sort of got it in my bones that something's going to happen."

"Same here, Ted," Dawson agreed. "I'm only half Scotch—mother's side—but maybe a half-Scot can be what my mother used to call 'fey'. You feel that you know, yet can't prove anything."

"That's it," Rapson nodded. "And I'm English, and Cockney at that! Sometimes I feel that I'd be glad if it 'ud happen and be done with, whatever it is."

Dawson laughed as he poured out a drink. "I reckon that Mr. Kebreau, if he's going to have another shot, will wait until he's got things all set. He won't risk another fiasco like the first one."

That was small comfort to Rapson.

To try to shake off the uneasy feeling he had, he threw himself vigorously into his work, found a further outlet for his energies in the frequent drilling in the evenings.

It was a day or so after his conversation with Dawson that Rapson heard the aeroplane, and saw it, a midge-like object flying at a great height on an east-to-west course. He was a mile or so from camp, finishing off the lay-out of a stretch of country through which the next section of the line was to be laid. He had with him only one or two natives, besides Jack Harley, one of his assistants.

"Somebody making a trans-continental flight," Harley suggested as Rapson straightened up from his theodolite and began to focus his glasses on the machine. "Make out its markings, sir?"

"No," Rapson answered. "Flying too high. But it's on a course that'll take it right over camp."

He watched the 'plane for a long time. Suddenly he said, harshly:

"It's going down, Jack!"

"Distinguished visitors!" Harley said, lightly.

"Don't be an ass," snapped Rapson. "It's not making for camp but for somewhere miles beyond. At any rate, that's what it looks like to me. You carry on as well as you can here. I'm going into camp. Hey, you!" he yelled at one of the natives, his gun-bearer. To venture out of camp without a gun would have been to court trouble, for there were wild animals of which to beware. "A 'plane landing anywhere up here, Jack," Rapson said, as the native came trotting up, "isn't a thing to pass up. I'm going to send or go out to try to find out something about it. S'long!"

"S'long, sir." Harley did not seem unduly impressed. "Reckon," he told himself as Rapson strode off "reckon he's got the jitters. Has had 'em ever since that trouble at Monrovia."

Rapson was like a wet rag when at last he reached

camp. He was also a worried man, because he knew that the aeroplane had landed somewhere, and then taken off again. He had lost sight of it, the sound of its engine had died away, and then, suddenly, there it was in the sky once more, cutting back on its course.

"Yes, sure, we saw and heard it," Dave Dawson told him, when he entered the office and asked a few questions. "I sent a couple of men out on a hand trolley with instructions to get off where they judged they were nearest the spot the machine must have landed at. That, I guess, was several miles north of the line. Soon after they left, the 'plane went up again. Ever see a place suitable for landing, Ted?"

"There are one or two out that way," Rapson answered. "Where's Lingard working?"

"Lingard—why?" Dawson frowned at the question.

"Why not?" Rapson countered. "Why shouldn't this mean that somebody's trying to get a message to him? You know darn well that everybody who comes up to camp is searched at Monrovia or wherever he gets on the train. Whites and natives alike. So nobody can bring in a written message. Verbal messages could be brought in, I know, but sometimes they're not satisfactory. So where's Lingard?"

"Let's go and see," was Dawson's suggestion. "As usual, Chalmers is working near him, and if Lingard had left his job, I'd have had word about it."

Alf Lingard was at work, tying down a stretch of the line, when Rapson and his companion strolled casually along, apparently making one of their frequent inspections. Rapson managed to get a few minutes with Chalmers, during which the latter informed him that Lingard had shown no greater interest in the aeroplane than had anyone else.

"Watch him!" was Rapson's final order as he walked away to rejoin Dawson. "I reckon," he told the latter, "that if somebody's been landed to meet Lingard, he'll either come into camp during the night or Lingard will go out to him. The latter'ud mean, of course, that the method had been settled beforehand, I rather favour the former."

"Why?" Dawson asked. They were sitting on a pile of rails, looking at the toiling humans. Away up, an excavator was scooping great feeds of earth out of a blasted hillock.

"Because after what happened when I accused Lingard of knowing where Kebreau was," said Rapson, "he'd know he'd have to be mighty careful of his movements. Absence from camp would be suspicious. Hello, he's in trouble!" Rapson broke off, as a Negro, clad only in dirty shorts, and carrying a number of shovels, stumbled over Lingard who was kneeling beside a fishplate. Lingard seemed to be smothered by shovels as he went down cursing, with the Liberian on top of him.

"Well, I'm hanged!" Ted Rapson seemed to be choking. He started up from the rails, then sat down again. "Did you see that, Dave?"

"See what?" Dawson asked.

"Something passed between that fellow and Lingard!" said Rapson quietly. "I saw something white, or I'm a dago!"

"I admit I didn't see it," Dawson said. The Liberian was on his feet by now, stooping to collect his scattered shovels. Lingard was up, too, and was continuing his vituperation of the man who, with a wide grin, set off along the line again.

"What about it, Ted?" Dawson asked, as Rapson made no move. "Aren't you going to bag the fellow— and Lingard, to make sure?"

"Got to be careful!" Rapson suggested. "Listen, Dave: you follow the Liberian, see where he goes, and get his number and name. Then arrange for tabs to be kept on him. I'm going to deal with Lingard. What? Why, doesn't it sound reasonable that if the fellow gave Lingard a message, he must either have been landed by that 'plane or been given it by someone who did land?"

"Gad, but you're right!" said Dawson. "Okay, Ted, I'll deal with him. Maybe the President was right and Lingard is going to lead to Kebreau."

"Hope so," was Rapson's parting shot as Dawson got up and walked casually along the line in the direction taken by the Liberian.

Rapson remained where he was, smoking, talking to men as they came by, but never missing a movement made by Lingard. It would have been a simple matter to call the man over at once, but Rapson preferred to leave him alone for a while, in order to lull him into confidence that the little passage between him and the Liberian had not attracted any more attention than that of amusement. He was not likely to look at the message he had received until he was alone. Moreover, Rapson did not wish to create trouble by tackling Lingard in the presence of the other workmen near by.

E

When, however, the break for the midday meal came, and Lingard moved off towards the long bunkhouse, Rapson followed him, wondering why Dawson had not returned. Rapson had lost sight of him long since, but was not really worried about him.

"Hey, Lingard!" Rapson hailed the beetle-browed man as he came past the pile of rails. Lingard stopped, and Rapson was sure of a momentary look of fear in his eyes. "Mind looking in at the office on the way in?" Rapson asked. "I shan't be able to get down for a while and want a message taken to Leader."

"Sure, sir," said Lingard, obviously relieved. Rapson handed him a sealed envelope, one of the usual kind, used to hold messages it was frequently necessary to send from place to place. Lingard slipped it into his trousers pocket, and with a nod, walked away. Rapson threw a glance over at Chalmers, who strolled casually from where he was working. As he passed Ted, the latter said, quietly:

"Keep him in sight. Better still, walk with him. I don't want him to open that letter!"

"Huh-huh!" came from Chalmers, who did not stop. Ted saw him gradually overhaul Lingard, and presently fall into step with him.

"Good enough!" Rapson grinned; and stayed where he was for a little longer. But at last he moved. Lingard and Chalmers were not in sight: they had got ahead of a crowd of natives. Rapson did not hurry; he wanted Lingard to be in the office when he arrived.

And Lingard was.

Chalmers, waiting outside, told Rapson so. Ted

walked in. Leader was writing. Lingard was sitting down, smoking a cigarette which Leader had given him.

"Hello—thought you weren't coming in, Ted," Leader exclaimed. "I was just writing a note for Lingard to give you when he went back to work."

"Changed my mind," Rapson said. "Shut the door, Chalmers."

Chalmers, who had followed him in, obeyed. He did not know what was afoot, but guessed something was going to break. He stood with his back to the door as Rapson walked over to where Lingard was sitting.

"Mind giving me the note that Negro passed to you, Lingard?"

Rapson spoke almost conversationally, but to the point. Lingard looked up at him.

"What the devil are you talkin' about?" he asked, and there was nothing beautiful about his face as he spoke. "What nigger?"

"The one who used shovels as though they were confetti," Rapson told him. "Come across, Lingard. I saw it! Where is——"

Lingard sprang to his feet, whipped up the bent-wood chair on which he had been sitting, and charged in with it at Rapson. Chalmers came rushing from the door. But Rapson ducked, went in under the chair, and took Lingard about the knees, jerked, and sent the fellow crashing down on his back. Lingard clung to the chair, however, and succeeded in smashing it up into Rapson's face as Ted was getting to his feet. Rapson staggered away—Lingard tried to rise, but Chalmers took him from the rear, wrenched away the chair which he flung across the room, and before Lingard could get up, fell on him and clamped him down to the floor by the neck.

Rapson recovered himself. Leader went in to help Chalmers, grabbed at one of Lingard's flailing legs and treated it in such a way that, but for the pressure on his throat, Lingard would have bellowed with pain. Rapson joined in the fray, but his objective was Lingard's pocket. The man was clad only in trousers and singlet: with two pockets in the former. From one of them, with an effort because Lingard twisted his body to try to prevent the hand coming out, Rapson wrenched something that was crumpled into a ball.

"Hold him!" he ordered, and smoothed out the ball. It was an envelope. Rapson ripped it open, ran his eyes over the sheet of paper which he drew out, then said: "Let him up—I've got what I wanted!"

Lingard came to his feet, his eyes glaring at Rapson from beneath his shaggy dark brows.

"By God, but you'll pay for this, Rapson!" he snarled.

Ted looked at him, a grim smile playing about his lips.

"Have you thought, Lingard," he said, "that as you joined the defence force and swore an oath to defend the railway, you've made yourself liable to punishment—I'm wondering how far the Liberian Government can really go, too! You're a damn traitor!"

"Bah—I'm an Englishman!" came from Lingard. "I——"

"I was never so sorry to hear a man say that as I am now," Rapson retorted. "Chalmers—get along, collect a few men and look for Dawson. No, wait a minute!" He stepped up to Lingard and seized him by his already aching throat. "Who are your pals?" he demanded. "Who else is working for Kebreau besides you?"

Lingard's answer was a vicious kick at Ted's shin, which made him hop and relax his grip. Lingard jerked free, turned for the door, reached it, and then went down, floored by the chair which Jim Leader sent hurtling at him.

After a fierce tussle he was secured again, and this time bound and flung into another room.

"He'll have to go down to Monrovia," said Rapson, panting. "I'll tell you chaps what's doing. Listen to this!" He pulled from his pocket the note he had taken off Lingard.

"I had to bring this myself, because I wanted to make sure you got it. Couldn't trust any of my men not to make a mistake. The day after to-morrow we shall hold up and take the supply train coming from Monrovia. It contains food and other stores, including dynamite, which we can do with. But we also need the train for transport purposes. The train at railhead will also be taken, in the following way. We shall bring up the captured supply train, with two hundred armed men aboard. They will have machine-guns, and we shall arrive at night to take the other train. If we meet with opposition we shall open fire. In the jungle there will be five hundred armed men, carrying extra weapons and ammunition. They are mostly natives recruited up country, with white officers. They will be put on the trains and we shall go down the line to pick up more men waiting for weapons. We shall carry on to Monrovia, about a thousand all told, and attack the

Government buildings again. Your part is to plant dynamite in camp, so that if there is a fight it will cause confusion. Tell the others to be ready with you to leave with us. Place dynamite with a time fuse to blow up the bridge after the trains are over, to prevent the defence force from crossing quickly enough. Your money will be ready for you in Monrovia. If you can smash up Rapson's machine do so. Watch for a smoke bomb from ours and you will know I have got away. K."

"Why, dammit all," Jim Leader exploded, "K must mean Kebreau!"

"Of course," Rapson nodded grimly. "It was Kebreau who brought the message and I sat and watched him, and didn't know! Get going, Chalmers. Find Dawson. I'm going down to the landing-ground to have my machine ready to take off! That 'plane's coming back to pick up Kebreau!"

CHAPTER VI

THE MAN WITH THE SCAR

DAVE DAWSON walked unhurriedly after he left Rapson. Ahead of him was the shovel-carrier, one of many men variously burdened. He was inconspicuous. Now and then he flung a word or two at other men but he did not stop walking. Dawson wondered whither the man was headed. Presently he knew. The Liberian cut away from the line and walked towards a supply depot. All manner of things were piled there, and beyond it, within a very few yards, lay the fringing jungle, which had had its seclusion and solitude broken by the iron road. Nobody took any notice of the Liberian as he reached the depot and threw down his shovels. Dawson, still some distance away, stopped to light his pipe. As he did so, he saw the man disappear round the great pile. Dave waited a few moments, but the Liberian did not show up. Dawson crossed the line, made for the depot, reached it, stood listening, but heard nothing. He eased around the depot and was just in time to see the Liberian disappearing into the jungle.

For the labourers to absent themselves and go into the jungle on occasion was no unusual thing, yet the present circumstances were such as to make Dawson suspicious. Nevertheless, because he did not want the Liberian to know that he had been followed, Dave

Dawson waited for a little while, to give the man time to return. For five minutes or so he waited, picking up and putting down several things, as if he were making a casual examination of them.

But the Liberian did not reappear, and Dawson grew worried. If Ted Rapson had been right, the fellow had delivered a message an hour or so after the arrival and departure of the mysterious aeroplane.

"The blighter's gone!" he muttered, presently, and strode towards the jungle. He had marked the tree near which he had last seen the Liberian. From it, he found it fairly easy to pick up the man's trail: trodden-down undergrowth, broken twigs here and there, were good enough signs for Dawson. After a while, he heard, when he stopped to listen, the sound of someone thrashing a way through the undergrowth, careless of the noise he made, and, as Dawson saw by the trail, taking no heed to that.

"Why the deuce didn't I bring my gun boy?" Dawson growled. "I've got only a revolver which wouldn't be much use if I met some big brute! But I guess I'm going right on, to see where this fellow's bound for!"

In contrast to his quarry, Dawson went cautiously: he had no desire for the Liberian to know that he was being followed. But the noise made by the man enabled Dawson to keep after him without any difficulty. Caution, however, was very necessary when, as happened now and then, the track lay on some animal trail. This made progress easier, but on the other hand, if Dawson had ventured too near, the

Liberian might have turned and seen him. At times the man's sounds ended; Dawson guessed he was resting, and was not sorry for the opportunity to do so himself. It was little past noon, and the heat was terrific, even in the forest, which acted as a shield from the direct rays of the sun.

Dawson, consulting his pocket compass, realized that the Liberian was making in the direction of the unknown place where the aeroplane had landed.

"But, hang it all," Dawson muttered, "would the 'plane come back to fetch a Negro workman? Having delivered his message, even if he'd been brought by 'plane, why wouldn't he be left to get away on his own, instead of risk being run with another landing? Or does it mean that wherever the place is, there is someone waiting to be told whether the message was delivered safely?"

That seemed to be sound argument, at least, and Dawson realized that he was perhaps up against a situation which might need more than one man to deal with. On the other hand, it was possible the Liberian belonged to one of the numerous villages in the district, places which would grow into towns as the result of the development that would follow the railway.

"Maybe that's all he's doing now, going home!" Dawson grinned. "But I'm going to try to find out!" He knew that the Government would take action against any such village if it could be proved that it was involved with Kebreau.

With conflicting ideas passing through his mind, Dave Dawson kept on the Liberian's trail.

He knew that they had covered several miles, gruelling, torturing miles, since they entered the jungle; and Dawson had not set eyes on the Liberian from the moment he disappeared amongst the trees. A wry smile came to Dawson's lips as he wondered what he would do if he came face to face with a Liberian there. He had not had a clear view of the man's face, and after all, one Negro, even in civilized Liberia, is much like another. There was no question of clothes helping towards identification: nearly all the men working on the line wore nothing else but shorts, and most of those were dirty.

"Haven't met anybody so far," Dawson grinned. "And I doubt whether the people who live around here often venture into the jungle, except to hunt, and then they come in bands. Anyway, if I see a Negro in dirty shorts I'm going to reckon he's the guy who stumbled over Lingard!"

He was enjoying one of the frequent rests just now, consequent on the cessation of his quarry's travelling sounds. But Dawson presently realized that this interval was considerably longer than any of the others had been. He waited a while longer, and then, when he heard nothing, decided it was up to him to do something. There was the possibility that the Liberian had realized he was being followed, though how he should have done, Dave was at a loss to understand. If he had, would he make off quietly, or would he not rather work back so that he could find out who was following? In that case, was he not likely to attack—if he had a weapon? Or even without one, since a surprise spring from the back might be expected to put his pursuer out of court without much further trouble.

Dawson resumed his journey, quietly, cautiously, following the undisguised trail left by his quarry.

He almost walked straight out of the jungle. The denseness of the undergrowth caused this. He only saved himself from doing so because he was suddenly aware of increased light. He pulled up, then walked carefully and slowly on: to find himself at the edge of the forest and looking out across a wide flat stretch of land, similar to many which he had come across while at work with Ted Rapson.

The alarming thing was that he had been, he reckoned, something like half a mile from the place when resting. That meant that his quarry had emerged from the jungle, instead of taking a rest! He had had time, therefore, to get across the level open country and to reach the hills beyond.

"Darn!" Dawson ground his teeth angrily as he realized that he seemed to have had his journey for nothing. "What the devil am I to do now?"

Was the Liberian still in the jungle, waiting for the return of the machine? Had the 'plane, indeed, made its landing here? At thought of this, Dawson pulled his binoculars round and took them from their case. Through them, he examined the ground beyond, but he did not find what he sought: long lines which a landing and taxi-ing machine would have made.

Dawson scrubbed thoughtfully at his chin. "Ted must have seen something, that's certain, otherwise how explain the Negro's actions? But no machine landed here, I'll swear." He examined the terrain again, but saw nothing to help him. Lowering the glasses, he smiled slowly. "I bet I know!" he muttered. "The 'plane landed at one place and if it's returning is landing at another one—here! Of course a second landing at the same place wouldn't be risked! I sent those two fellows out on a wild-goose chase!"

It seemed a reasonable idea. But where was the Liberian? Was he waiting in the jungle, or had he, after all, only come this way because it led to a village whither he had succeeded in going, or at least had managed to cover the open stretch of country? Dawson wished he knew what was in the message. Was it of such importance that it was necessary for whoever had sent it to know that it had been delivered? If so, then the 'plane would be coming.

Dawson started suddenly, and looked round. There were movements to his left.

He could not see anything. He pressed against the nearest tree, revolver in hand. The movements continued, but they were not those of someone approaching the spot where he stood hidden by the thick bole of a tree. Presently they ceased, but others followed: footfalls these, without any accompaniment of swishing undergrowth.

Looking out, Dave Dawson saw a shorts-clad man walking away from the forest. He was carrying a great bundle of herbage.

For the first time Dawson, not more than ten feet away, and nearer than he had yet been to the man, got a clear view of his face. The Liberian was walking sidewise to Dawson, his right profile clearly visible.

For a moment or two Dawson stood there, staring in almost utter disbelief.

"Good God!" he gasped, at last, then clapped a hand over his mouth, as if to stifle the sound which he felt sure must have carried to the Liberian. "Kebreau himself!"

There was no mistaking the man: Dawson had met him, had seen the hideous scar which stretched from the man's right ear in a curve along his jaw-bone. It had shrivelled up the right side of the Liberian's face.

"Kebreau himself!" Dawson breathed the words again, and raised his revolver as he did so.

CHAPTER VII

DISASTER

EVEN as his finger curled about the trigger of the revolver, Dave Dawson lowered the weapon.

He could have shot down Kebreau before the would-be President of Liberia knew anyone was near. It was not that Dawson could not bring himself to shoot an unsuspecting man. This, after all, was war, and the death of Kebreau would probably save the lives of many people. But this did not, in the heat of the moment, enter Dawson's mind, as later he admitted to Rapson. What saved Kebreau's life just then was that Dave realized that the Liberian was there to await the arrival of the aeroplane. Dawson believed the herbage was being taken to make a signal fire, a pre-arranged signal, by which the pilot would know either that the message had been delivered or that Kebreau wanted to be picked up, and that it was safe for the machine to land. Which was the real answer did not trouble Dawson, except that if the 'plane landed, he might get a chance to do something.

"I'll give Kebreau his head," he murmured. "Maybe he's going to build more than one fire—I should, instead of relying on a single one which anybody might think of! I can get him just when I want to—and I may be able to snaffle the machine and pilot as well. Gad! What a break!"

He watched Kebreau carry his bundle to a considerable distance and put it on the ground. Then the Liberian went into the jungle again, but to Dawson's alarm, at a point a long way off! Dave, however, durst not move yet, in case Kebreau, who would perhaps be alert, saw him. Kebreau actually took five heaps of fuel and, through his glasses, Dawson saw that they were arranged in the shape of an enormous "X".

It was then that Dawson knew that Kebreau had finished his fuel-carrying, and did not intend to return to the jungle. The unsatisfactory aspect of this for Dawson was that the heaps were a considerable distance away, and for him to get near enough to fire with any chance of hitting his mark, it would be necessary to make a trip along the jungle-edge.

He was making this journey, with Kebreau unseen as he lay under cover from the sun in the shade of one of his unlighted fires, when he heard the distant drone of an engine. He moved close to the edge of the forest, in order to see what Kebreau would do.

Through his glasses he saw the Liberian standing beside the centre-piece of his letter "X", shielding his eyes with his hand and looking up into the sky. A moment or so later, he set light to the pile of scrub and went across to another. Dawson, from his position, could not see the aeroplane, the sound of whose engine was growing louder each second—until it became a terrific roar.

Then the machine swum into Dawson's vision, as all five fires sent up flames and smoke. Straight up they went, for there was no wind, not even a zephyr breeze to cool the air. Dawson knew that, widely spaced as the fires were, the formation of the "X" would be observable from the aeroplane, which suddenly went into a loop. Dawson took that to be a signal to Kebreau, for immediately afterwards the 'plane made a circling journey, its engine throttled down, and Dawson saw that the machine was coming down.

And Kebreau was over half a mile away from where Dawson was standing.

"I've got to get closer!" he grated, and resumed his journey through the jungle. He knew he would be able to come within a quarter of a mile of Kebreau if he had time. Then he meant to take a chance and fire—immediately the machine landed. He reckoned that if he brought down Kebreau the pilot would get out to help him, and thus present himself as a second target. Dawson had identified the 'plane as a Heinkel, token that Kebreau still had his non-Liberian friends.

"Dammit!" Dawson snapped, as the machine landed, long before he had reached the position for which he was making. He stopped, saw that the 'plane had landed between him and Kebreau. "A devil of a mess!" he growled. "But thank heaven Ted's no fool! He'll surely be expecting something like this to happen, and he'll have his machine ready, I'll bet! But what the devil do I have to do? Perhaps I ought to have downed Kebreau when I could have done!"

The only view now that he had of Kebreau was through the gap between the 'plane and the ground as the Liberian came running up. The fellow was

DAWSON HAD IDENTIFIED THE 'PLANE AS A HEINKEL

Facing page 80.

an impossible target at the distance. Pot-shots at the machine itself would almost certainly be useless; even bullets put through the tail, which he felt he could manage, would not be certain to make take-off impossible. And Dave Dawson knew the seriousness of failure on his part.

"Even if I got away," he muttered, "the very fact that they were attacked would tell them Kebreau's visit to camp was discovered! The message must be darned important to justify Kebreau's bringing it. As I'm not likely to be able to stop 'em, I'd better do nothing. Dammit all!"

It was maddening to know that he was impotent to do anything to stop Kebreau from getting away. He hoped, almost prayed, that Ted Rapson would go up; the noise of the machine must have been heard in camp. Dawson realized, however, that unless Rapson had foreseen the return of the aeroplane, and gone down to the landing-ground, which was a mile or so along the line, he would stand little, if any, chance of preventing Kebreau from escaping. If the Heinkel took off quickly, there would be no over-taking it—no chance, even, of knowing where it was going. That the intention was not to remain here was evident to Dawson, because the Heinkel's engine was turning over while Kebreau was approaching.

It was a great temptation when, a few minutes later, he saw the Liberian clearly. Kebreau had reached the machine and was climbing up.

"My God—ought I?" Dawson rasped, and then was aware of a sound as of far-off thunder. He could have whooped for very relief. "I'll bet that's Ted

F

in the Moth!" he breathed. "What the devil shall
I do, though?"

He had no chance to do anything, however, for
Kebreau was in the Heinkel. The engine roared to
life, and the machine went taxiing away.

"I'll bet the pilot saw the Moth before ever he
landed!" Dawson grated. "That's why he didn't
shut off his engine and stayed down only long enough
to allow Kebreau to get in!"

Dawson, however, felt much better.

"That must be Rapson coming!" he grinned.
"Maybe he's seen Kebreau's message—but I'll bet
he doesn't know it was Kebreau who brought it!"
He scanned the brazen sky through his glasses and
presently picked out the Moth—and wondered what
was going to happen next.

The Heinkel was climbing rapidly. The Moth was
still a long way off, but was coming down in a roaring
dive, obviously with the intention of engaging the
Heinkel before the latter could reach any height.
Tense with excitement, Dawson watched, saw the
Heinkel go into a zoom, flatten out presently, and
drive forward at speed, only to zoom once more.
These tactics caused the Moth to pull out of its dive
and change course.

It was like watching a game of hide and seek played
in the sky to the accompaniment of roaring engines
and, presently, with machine-guns in action.

Dawson could see the grey smoke of the tracers
slashing through the air. Wheeling, rolling, diving,
climbing—the two machines looked like giant vultures
fighting over carrion they had scented or seen.

"Good old Ted!" Dawson yelled, as if he expected Rapson to hear him. "Go to it, boy! Gad, but he can handle that Moth! I suppose it's Leader he's got with him. Darn good job we fixed that machine-gun!"

Even as he was exulting over the way in which the Moth was being fought, the end came suddenly, tragically—for Dave Dawson.

The Moth, revolving as it were round a centre that was the Heinkel, stopped firing.

The only tracers Dawson could see were those spewing from the Heinkel's gun. Then the Moth shot off at a tangent and climbed, the Heinkel after it.

"Bet the machine-gun's jammed, or Leader's killed!" Dawson choked. "If it's the gun, Ted's flying away to give Leader time for it to be put right. If Jim's finished—God! So will Ted be, unless a miracle happens. He can't use the gun and fly the machine!"

Long since, Dawson had come out of the jungle. He stood, neck aching, gazing up. As he watched, he experienced a revulsion of feeling; he wished that he had obeyed the impulse to shoot Kebreau. It would have saved Rapson and whoever was in the Moth with him. But regret was useless. Dawson could only stand there, his eyes following the machines, praying for the moment to come when the Moth's machine-gun would spurt bullets once more. But that did not happen, and the Moth kept climbing. It had been to its advantage that it was much higher than the Heinkel, but the latter was now climbing rapidly.

Dawson saw that the Moth was heading in the direction of the camp. He was thankful for that much. If Rapson could make camp, the Heinkel, unless it was carrying bombs, would be unable to do much damage there. True, it could dive and machine-gun the workmen, but it would be met by machine-guns and rifles; the defence force would not take an attack lying down. Dawson felt sure that Ted would have given orders before he left for the defence force to be ready for whatever might happen.

Dave saw the Moth top the range of hills, saw the Heinkel hard on its tail: then he lost sight of both machines, but could still hear the thunder of their engines.

"Back for me!" he grated. "God help Ted!" and he ran towards the jungle, dashed along its edge until at last he reached the spot whence he had first looked out on to the plain. "I'll be able to follow the back trail all right, I reckon!" he muttered as he plunged into the forest. "Why the devil didn't I shoot Kebreau?"

CHAPTER VIII

DILEMMA

TED RAPSON and Jim Leader hurried from the office. They went down to the biggest bunkhouse.

"Listen men!" Rapson's voice sounded above the noise of chattering, laughing men. Silence fell immediately, and all eyes were turned on him as he stood in the doorway. Ted tried to get a quick, comprehensive register of the men: he remembered what the letter had said about "the others," and although none of these knew what had happened to Lingard, accomplices might assume that the obvious concern of Rapson had its cause in their machinations. But Rapson failed to notice anything suspicious about any of the men. He had no intention of broadcasting the news about the letter, but he did intend to have the men ready for any emergency.

"As soon as you've finished," he said, "work will be resumed under arms."

A buzz of excitement ran through the bunkhouse, and the men looked curiously at Rapson, who went on:

"I have reason to believe that the aeroplane which was seen a little while ago will be coming back, and that it belongs to Kebreau, the rebel."

"Strewth, boss, does that mean we're goin' to be bombed?" a voice asked.

"If that had been the intention," Rapson answered,

grimly, "the bombing would have taken place before this, I think. No, there's another explanation, which I'm not at liberty to give at the moment. I am going to have my machine ready to take off if the other 'plane does come back. That may mean a fight up there," he jerked a thumb upwards, significantly. "If I lose—well, perhaps the enemy may fancy a farewell attack. Machine-gunning, for instance. So that's why I want the defence force ready. Denny!" One of the men, an engine-driver, stood up. "I want you to have your engine ready to leave if it should happen that one or other of the machines is forced down anywhere along the line. You'll set off with a squad of men. All this, of course," he added, "is merely precautionary and there may be no need for anything to be done."

The prospect of a fight had seemed to please the men. Rapson's suggestion that there might not be one appeared to disappoint them. Rapson was, however, quite content: he knew that if occasion arose the men would fight. He left the bunkhouse with Jimmy Leader and hurried to a siding where a hand-trolley was standing. He put off the brakes and both men pushed the trolley until it had gained sufficient speed; then they sprang on to it, and, working the handles, set off down line.

They were bathed in perspiration when they reached the landing-field, but they lost no time in fuelling the aeroplane, oiling it, and taking several drums of ammunition on board for the machine-gun.

"All set, Jimmy," Rapson grinned. "If the Heinkel shows up, we'll be after it."

"Okay, Ted," said Leader. "I've been wondering why you haven't advised Monrovia, though."

"Monrovia couldn't do anything up here in time, if the 'plane returns," said Rapson. "But I've told Chalmers, if anything happens to us," he glanced at his companion, but there was no sign of fear, "he's to get in touch with Monrovia and tell exactly what's in Kebreau's letter. Chalmers has got it. I wish to heaven I knew what had happened to Dawson!"

"That looks obvious to me," said Leader. "He's followed Kebreau, even if he doesn't know the messenger is Kebreau. He may have discovered that fact too late to be able to find a man to send back with the news."

It was small consolation to Rapson. Dave Dawson was more than a colleague: he was a friend. He was also a fearless man, and Ted knew he would not let up on Kebreau's trail, even at risk of losing his own life. Rapson therefore spent the next hour or so filled with anxiety and hoping that Dawson would put in an appearance. Instead of Dawson, however, Maystone, one of the men sent by hand-trolley, arrived. Ted saw the man working the trolley furiously and when he was near the landing-field he hailed him. Maystone pulled up.

"Where's Simmonds?" Rapson asked.

"Left him away back, sir," was the answer. "We've found the place where a machine landed—there were wheel-tracks and foot-prints. I left Simmonds to watch and was going up to report."

"Carry on!" snapped Ted. "Tell Cleaver to take some men down on the train and—God! It's too late!'' he exclaimed, as he heard the drone of an aeroplane. Through his glasses he presently saw the machine, decided it was the Heinkel, and knew that it would take him some time to reach the height at which it was flying.

"Did you see Dawson?" he rapped the question at Maystone.

"Dawson—why, no, sir," was the answer.

"Nor anybody else—anybody apparently waiting?" Ted asked, and Maystone shook his head.

They were having to yell at each other, because Leader had opened up the engine of the Moth. Rapson told Maystone to get to camp and give instructions for men to be taken to the landing place where Simmonds was waiting. Then he ran up to the Moth. He climbed into the front cockpit. Leader was behind, with the fixed machine-gun mounted at his side.

"It's a bit of a mess, Jim!" Rapson said, throttling down. "If we go up now Kebreau may take fright and clear off—and chance being able to make a get-away by some other means. On the other hand, if we wait, the Heinkel will be able to take him off. Maystone hasn't seen Dave, which may mean all kinds of things! Darned if I know what to do."

"I'd suggest," said Leader, "that we wait until the Heinkel looks as if it's going to land. Then go up—and meet it as it's climbing again. It'll have Kebreau aboard—unless Dave has been able to do something to the fellow."

"That's a good idea, Jimmy," Rapson nodded. "All right—we'll stay put for a while and see what happens."

What did happen was that the Heinkel, which flew

at a great height for a while, suddenly changed course somewhat, and then its engine died.

"Going down!" grated Rapson, and opened his throttle. The 'plane shot across the landing-field, took off—and was on the way to whatever was awaiting it.

Rapson climbed swiftly. He saw, at a great distance, the gliding Heinkel, and presently realized that it was making for a wide stretch of open country.

"That's not the place Maystone spoke about!" he told Leader. "Looks as if Kebreau was landed at one spot and arranged to be picked up at another. Which doesn't sound unreasonable, after all!"

The Heinkel landed. Rapson saw it streaking along the ground, from which rose five columns of smoke. Presently the 'plane stopped and an ant-like figure ran towards it. Anxiously, Rapson scanned the ground, hoping to see some sign of another man— Dawson. But he saw nothing more than the smoke, the Heinkel, and the running figure, which he knew must be Kebreau.

"Nobody's getting out of the Heinkel!" Ted shouted to Leader. "Probably we've been seen and it's a case for a quick take-off. Yes, that's it! Look—Kebreau's in!"

He pushed the stick forward and the Moth's nose went down. Rapson was going into action in a roaring dive. He hoped to give Leader a chance at the Heinkel before it could take off. But in this he was disappointed: the Heinkel streaked across the ground and took off, climbed rapidly, flattened out and drove forward. Then it zoomed and Rapson knew the pilot was trying to snatch height. Rapson changed course, came over the Heinkel which was zooming again. Leader opened out with his machine-gun. The Heinkel flattened out and roared away, the Moth after it. Tracers slashed between the two machines as Rapson succeeded in retaining height over the Heinkel. He made circles around it. The machine-guns spewed their death-missiles, some of which found marks on fuselage and cabin-covers.

Then, suddenly, Rapson was conscious that Leader was not firing. He turned and saw his companion slumped forward in the cockpit, blood pouring from his head.

"God! They've got him!" Rapson snarled, and realized that the fight was over as far as he was concerned. The fixed machine-gun was useless for him; he could not work it from the front cockpit. He registered a decision that, if he came out of this scrap alive, he would have a gun fitted for the pilot. Meanwhile, he knew, with chagrin in his soul, that the only thing for him to do was to pound away . . . defeated. . . . Leaving Kebreau free to go.

"No, darn it!" Rapson gritted. "I'm going to do something—I'll try and lure the Heinkel over camp. Perhaps they'll dive for me and then the men can have a go at them!"

He swung out of the fight and put the Moth at full speed. He was still higher than the Heinkel which went roaring after him, its machine-gun pouring bullets, the 'plane climbing all the time. Now and then Ted glanced round hoping to see Leader showing signs of life: but Leader was still slumped forward and there was nothing Ted could do for him.

The Heinkel got the height. It had lost way slightly in doing so, but now it pelted after the Moth. For his part, Rapson was roaring down towards the camp. He could see the engine, steam and smoke issuing from it; and those tiny dots were men.

The Moth passed the camp. The Heinkel spewed bullets down at the machine. Rapson turned and went back, this time right over the camp, from which, as yet, no firing had come. Now, as Ted, with an engine that roared thunderously, dived and swept over camp, the Heinkel, a little behind, was subjected to brisk fire from rifles and machine-guns of men in whatever cover they had been able to find. Ted Rapson grinned to himself as he saw a vast amount of smoke coming from the engine which was on the move. As it travelled, the smoke spread and formed a screen. Backwards and forwards the engine went and, judging by the smoke produced, whoever was firing was working overtime feeding the furnace with wood.

Suddenly the engine stopped its running to and fro and went pounding down the line. Rapson guessed that the driver had realized the Moth was in trouble; the very fact that its machine-gun was not answering the fire from the Heinkel would prove that.

Rapson was ahead of the engine when it started. The Heinkel, after diving low and being met by a brisk fire, had climbed. Now it was pursuing the engine, as if the pilot felt that it held some menace. Looking behind, Rapson saw the engine being machine-gunned, but it was speeding down the line. There were two trucks behind it, and Rapson saw men leaping from them and scurrying for cover.

"Looks to me," grated Rapson, "as if Denny's trying to tell me to make for the landing-field. Perhaps he's got someone on board who will work the machine-gun—if I can land and take off!"

He reckoned that it was known down below that either the gun had jammed or Leader been put out of action. But there seemed little possibility of the Moth being able to land and take a new gunner aboard —with the Heinkel worrying around like an angry hornet. Yet Rapson resolved to make the attempt; and since the Heinkel was devoting its attention to the engine, he succeeded in making a safe landing and was helping out an unconscious, but living, Jimmy Leader before the enemy 'plane came over.

And when it came, it did nothing except make a circling of the field, then fly towards the Moth as if intending to machine-gun it instead of which, something struck the ground not far from the 'plane— and then the Heinkel was climbing and heading northwards.

At first, Rapson thought a bomb had been dropped. He knew, however, that it was unlikely, because if the Heinkel had been carrying bombs it would, surely, have dropped some before this. Also, whatever it was, did not explode.

Rapson saw men running up from the line, where the engine had just stopped. He laid Leader on the ground and climbed back into the machine to get out the first-aid kit. He was back with Leader when the men arrived.

"What happened, sir?" one of them asked. "Leader dead?"

"No, fortunately," Rapson answered. "Either of you fellows likely to be able to handle a machine-gun in the 'plane?"

"I'll bet I can, sir!" a man named Fawden stepped out.

Rapson tossed him a key.

"You and some others get some petrol from the store, there!" he said. "I'll attend to Leader. The gun's all right. I'm going after the Heinkel if we can fuel up quickly!"

But by the time the Moth had been fuelled, Ted Rapson realized that pursuit was impossible. Long since, the sound of the Heinkel had died away. He knew that the machine could have changed course could, indeed, have made a landing many miles away before this. He was puzzled over its retreat, and after having brought Leader back to consciousness —Jim had got a knock-out blow by a bullet across his head—Rapson began to search the landing-field. He found, presently, what he sought: an empty ammunition drum.

"That's the explanation," he told the men. "Kebreau tossed that out just to let us know why he didn't stay to smother the Moth with bullets here. He'd run out of ammo!"

Fawden cursed somewhat. "Isn't that rotten luck! We could perhaps have downed him. He's got the devil's own luck, I reckon!"

"Even that'll run out, I reckon," said Rapson. "Where's Denny, by the way?"

"Dead, sir!" was the answer. "He got a bullet when he shoved his head out of the cab—fellows were jumping off because of the machine-gunning. Some of us stayed, a few were wounded, and a couple killed. Several casualties up in camp, too. No, sir, Dawson hasn't shown up yet."

"Looks rather as though Kebreau found out he was being followed," Rapson said, harshly. "Perhaps he managed to get Dave!"

This was a perturbing thought. For one thing, if Kebreau had discovered his trailer and turned on him, then Rapson had lost a good colleague and a fine friend. For another, Kebreau would know that it had been found out that he delivered a message at the camp. That, in itself, would tell him that his plans were probably known. The fact of the Moth's having gone up after the Heinkel would not, alone, have suggested this discovery: Kebreau was clever enough to realize that an apparently aimless coming and going of a strange 'plane would, in the circumstances, put the railway workers on the *qui vive*: it was to be expected that they would not be unprepared for a further visit. Indeed, as Rapson looked at matters, Kebreau would almost certainly reckon on the appearance of a Heinkel being regarded with suspicion and as the forerunner of further activities on the part of the disaffected elements in Liberia. The Moth's joining issue with the Heinkel need not necessarily therefore have any link with Kebreau's visit to camp. But if Dawson had fallen down on his tracking of Kebreau, then the whole aspect of affairs was altered.

Ted Rapson was in thoughtful mood as, with Leader made comfortable on the train, he rode back to camp.

"We've got to do something," he told Chalmers on arrival. "I'm going to advise Monrovia as soon as I've written out a message in code. Let me have another look at Kebreau's letter."

After reading it, he sat down and re-wrote it in the code given him by President Coolidge.

"Trouble is, Chalmers," he said, presently, "that we don't know where Kebreau intends to hold-up the supply train the day after to-morrow. If we did, it could be arranged to have a force there. Another thing is, we don't know where those armed recruits are coming from, heading towards camp. I can try to do something on that point, however. To-morrow I'll make a wide survey of the country and endeavour to locate them, although the odds are on them keeping to the jungle. Darned if I know what to do!"

"Better let Monrovia do the worrying," Chalmers suggested.

"I don't know yet," Rapson countered. "I'm going to wait and see whether Dawson turns up. If he does, and he's certain that Kebreau wasn't wise to him, then I think I can see a way out."

They were in the frame building which served as living quarters to Rapson and a few other men. Leader was lying in his bed, obviously in a fever as the result of his wound. Doctor Colling had, however, assured Rapson that it was nothing more serious than a slight concussion.

"A creased skull," he said. "Leader will be all right, you can be sure of that."

Briscoe, the assistant telegraphist, came in.

"Seems as if the line's broken down, sir," he reported.

"I was receiving. There was a sudden stop. I tried to contact but couldn't."

"Not unlikely!" said Rapson with a grim smile. "If Kebreau isn't sure how things stand as far as our knowledge is concerned, he'd be bound to cut the wires. We'll send the breakdown gang out to see if they can locate the fault. I daresay Monrovia will do the same from that end."

CHAPTER IX

RECONNAISSANCE FLIGHT

RAPSON was in the general room used by the staff when Dave Dawson arrived. Work had ceased for the day, and the African night had fallen while Dawson was still in the jungle. It had been a terrifying experience for him until he emerged. Fear had been with him lest he should have had to spend the night in the forest. He knew also another fear: that Rapson might have come to grief. He did not know that Ted had passed safely through the encounter with the Heinkel, nor that he had sent out search-parties which had had to give up before the sudden nightfall, without having picked up the trail Dawson and Kebreau had taken.

Simmonds had been brought in from where Maystone left him; and all he had to report was that he had heard, from a long distance, the sound of aero-engines, but had seen nothing of the machines. Rapson knew for certain, then, that the Heinkel had landed at two widely separated spots. This served to make him more concerned than ever regarding Dawson, and it was with considerable relief that he saw Dave enter the room.

"Thank God you're safe!" Rapson cried and grabbed Dave by the hand. Dawson was a big man and strong, but his endurance had been strained during the past hours.

"For Lord's sake, give me a drink, Ted!" he gasped, and flopped into a chair. "Yes, as stiff as you like!" as Ted, pouring whisky into the glass, looked inquiringly at him. Dawson downed the drink avidly. "Do you know," he said, smacking his lips, "that I haven't had a drink for three hours? I didn't start out with anything, as you know—wasn't expecting to leave the job, of course. I found a little stream coming back. Filthy water, but I had a go at it and soaked a couple of handkerchiefs in the stuff, and sucked 'em now and again. Well, what's been happening?"

"You lost Kebreau then?" Rapson asked, with a twisted smile. If he thought he was giving Dawson a surprise, he was mistaken, and knew so at once.

"So you found out the fellow was Kebreau?" Dawson grinned. "How?"

For answer, Rapson flicked over the letter, which Dawson read quickly.

"An enterprising rebel, Ted," he said, as he gave back the note. "I followed the blighter right through the jungle, and then missed him for a while." He explained everything then, adding: "I suppose you didn't get him, Ted?"

"No, darn him!" growled Rapson. "Why the devil didn't you——"

"Ted, old man," said Dawson, almost humbly, certainly apologetically, "I wish to heaven I'd plugged the swine. But I thought—and I was right—that he'd give a signal. If I shot him, he wouldn't be able to do that, and the Heinkel wouldn't land. So I waited. I thought if the Heinkel showed up, as it seemed to me it was bound to, you'd take off in the Moth. I reckoned on getting a shot at Kebreau if the Heinkel landed while you were diving down for it. In that way, we'd have got Kebreau and his pilot and his 'plane. But"—he shrugged his shoulders, and held out his glass to Rapson—"I reckon things went all goofy, Ted! But please don't rub it in because I made a mistake in judgment. Can I ask why you——"

"Ran away?" Rapson jerked. "Yes, you can, Dave! I had to, because poor old Jimmy—— No, not that!" he said, in answer to the monosyllabic question which came from Dawson. "Not killed, but wounded. I couldn't use the machine-gun, so just had to bunk for it."

Dawson emptied a jugful of water. "What you'd call a winning day for Kebreau, Ted! What're we going to do? You say the wires have been cut, so I suppose you'll fly down to Monrovia and take in Lingard?"

Rapson laughed harshly. "Alf Lingard's skipped it."

"What!" jerked Dawson. "You told me you'd left him trussed up!"

"So I did," Rapson said. "But somebody cut him free—during the commotion here. Remember what the letter said, Dave? 'The others!' There are others in Kebreau's pay and one of 'em turned Lingard loose. May have given him a gun and grub. Lingard will stay around until the day after to-morrow when he'll hope to be able to join the rebels who're coming here."

"Had Lingard read Kebreau's letter?" Dawson asked, suddenly.

"The envelope was sealed when I got it from him," Rapson answered. "So he couldn't know about the armed men due here. I'd overlooked that point, Dave."

"It raises another interesting one, Ted," Dawson said. "How many of us know the contents of the letter? Did you tell the men about it?"

"No!" Rapson admitted. "All I told them was that I believed the machine which came over first belonged to Kebreau and that it probably meant something was brewing. Therefore we'd better be prepared. I purposely left it as vague as that."

"One of 'the others'," said Dawson, "must have seen Lingard come into the office, but not go out again, and guessed that something was wrong. That's why he released Lingard. But my point is this, Ted: unless you yourself go down to Monrovia, or let me go, in the 'plane, we really don't know whom we can trust. Even if the telegraph line is repaired, there's the question, may there not be a traitor at the other end? If we send the train down, may not the line have been torn up?"

"Not that, I think," said Rapson. "Remember, Kebreau reckons on bringing up the supply train. He'd have to wreck both lines to stop us from sending down a train. But what are you trying to get at?"

"That we may be able to put the kybosh on Kebreau without asking for help from Monrovia," was the answer. "If we told Monrovia, what would happen?"

"Troops would be sent up the line," Rapson asserted. "But they wouldn't know where to wait for the proposed hold-up."

"Exactly," Dawson nodded, with a grim smile on his face. "And the very fact of troops being sent out would tell Kebreau's spies that his plan was known. He'd be likely to postpone it until he could bring off a coup by surprise."

"Lingard's escaped," Rapson reminded him.

Dawson nodded. "But he doesn't know where the hold-up's planned to take place or where the army from up-country is—at any rate, I imagine he doesn't. It's something for us to take a chance on. I've got a scheme, if you'd care to listen to it?"

"Let's have it!" snapped Ted.

"We'll carry on as though nothing had happened," Dawson said. "Except that you might make an aerial survey trip to-morrow—there'll be nothing unusual in that. You might spot a concentration of men. Even if you don't, but they see you, they're more than likely to believe you're out on your—er—lawful occasions, if I may use a naval term! If you do— well, we might find it possible, supposing they're near, to attack them. If you don't, we can arrange for some of our force to stay here on the fateful night to defend camp. But the train will go down the line with as many armed men as we can afford. We'll go a distance of only a few miles, and there tear up part of the track so that the supply train can't proceed."

"You mean," Rapson frowned, "that we allow Kebreau to seize it?"

"Seems the only way," Dawson admitted. "But it will have to stop at the broken track. That's where we'll come in! Our train will have steamed back— we'll be hidden, waiting; and then I reckon it'll be a case of leaving it to the gods."

"It would certainly mean, if we were lucky," said

Rapson, "that we should prevent the two rebel forces meeting. Yes, there's something in the idea, Dave. But we'll keep mum about it until the last minute, in case!"

"Yes, in case 'the others' may have a way of getting in touch with Kebreau or some of his crowd," Dawson agreed. "And now I'd like nothing better than sleep. Going to post sentries, Ted?"

"You bet!" was the immediate answer. "I'd already settled that, Dave! And I'm going down to the landing-field to sleep in the 'plane, so that I shall be ready if General Kebreau takes it into his head to visit us during the night. Fawden's going to be with me. He can use a machine-gun, so he says. Sure, but not to-night, Dave. You've got to get some rest after what you've gone through!"

Dawson did not demur, after a quick protest that he ought to take Fawden's place down at the flying-field, and Rapson went away. He was so tired that, despite his anxiety, despite the knowledge that there were traitors in camp, he fell alseep almost as soon as he sat down in his cockpit.

Fawden kept vigil—and remained on guard for a double spell, rather than disturb Rapson. Ted, in due course, however, took Fawden's post, but the vigil was quite unnecessary, and dawn broke at last without anything untoward having taken place.

At breakfast, Rapson said to Dawson: "I reckon you'd better stay in camp, Dave. I'll take Fawden up with me, in case there's any trouble and the machine-gun has to be used! As second-in-command you'll have full authority."

"You're the boss," Dawson grinned. "I'm hoping that by the time you come in we'll have the mounting ready for a second machine-gun. If you do spot a concentration of men, it's almost bound to be Kebreau's crowd. What'll you do? Attack?"

"Almost certain isn't quite!" said Rapson. "I'd hate to drop bombs amongst innocent natives—and it'ud be difficult to be sure. I'll have to wait and see what happens. Telegraph's all right again, so I was told, as I came up."

"Yes—break-down gang from Monrovia did it," Dawson said. "Long stretches of wire removed— Monrovia thinks natives did it for the usual ornaments! I didn't let on about what had happened up here and Monrovia had nothing to report."

"Kebreau's not working from Monrovia," Rapson suggested. "There are many places he could use as headquarters. I hope to goodness we're doing right, Dave, keeping things to ourselves. If we're not— tchk! There'll be trouble a-plenty. If, however, we have any luck, I really believe we shall prevent a bloody business. I mean, prevent Kebreau from marching on Monrovia and creating civil war. Anyway, I'm going to take a chance."

"Stout feller!" Dawson commented, and Ted went out to pick up Fawden and make for the waiting aeroplane.

"Up-country may mean anything, Fawden," Ted said, as they allowed the engine to warm up. "So we'll just make a trip on the hit-and-miss principle."

"Yes, sir," Fawden agreed. He had been taken completely into Rapson's confidence. "I suppose there's no chance of Lingard getting in with a warning?"

"Not unless he had been previously informed of the proposed concentration of men and where it would take place," Rapson answered. "All set?" he asked, and a few seconds later the Moth was on its way across the field. It took off cleanly, and Ted chose his course along the route of the railway as far as completed. Then he continued over the cleared country being prepared for further building, and so above the forest where gangs of labourers were toiling, felling trees, dynamiting the stumps and leaving a wholesale mess for the excavators to shift.

Beyond this, the Moth flew, as if on a survey of untouched country. It was not the first time, by any means, that Rapson had made this flight: he had made it on several occasions during which the aerial-photographic survey was in progress. He had photographed from the air most of the range of hills some twenty-five miles from camp, and as the result the route had been selected. Now, he made a flight in ever-widening circles over the hills, realizing that such a place was ideal for the encamping of several hundred men. He did not expect to see them in concentration, but there was the chance that small groups, engaged in any one of a hundred kind of jobs, might show up.

"Say, boss, what's that on the river over there?" Fawden bawled his question at Rapson without taking his binoculars down. Ted was not unprepared for the question, because he, too, had been looking at the river. Rapson knew the river, whereas Fawden did not and, therefore, was unaware of the existence of a native bamboo bridge which was stretched between the banks. At the height the Moth was flying, the bridge was rather like a scratch on a shimmering surface, but Rapson presently made out men moving along it. On both banks there were other men, some waiting to step on, others who had stepped off and were forming up to march away.

"We're in luck!" Rapson shouted, but he did not change course in order to pass over the river. He flew straight on, and left the river on his left. He knew where he was going and what he intended to do. Three miles beyond the hills, through which the river ran, was ground suitable for landing: Rapson had landed there before this. He throttled down his engine after passing the spot, flying a couple more miles and turning back. The distance would have killed the sound of his engine, and the 'plane would not be seen as it glided towards the earth.

He grounded the machine safely, and got out.

"Kebreau may be with that crowd," he told Fawden. "We could have dropped some bombs amongst them and scattered them, but it would have given away the fact that we know about the plot for to-morrow. Also, if Kebreau's there, he might escape the death he deserves. So I've decided to go on foot to see if we can locate their camp. By starting from the bridge I ought to be able to follow the trail."

"Where do I come in, sir?" Fawden asked.

"You'll come with me," Rapson grinned. "First, however, we're going to camouflage the 'plane as best we can."

They did it by tearing down branches of trees and carrying them to where the machine was stood; they piled the branches on the 'plane in sufficient quantities until Rapson knew that unless anyone came up quite close they would take it for a big patch of scrub. Even if the Heinkel were in the neighbourhood and flew over, the Moth would be unidentifiable from above.

The spot chosen by Rapson was on the near side of the river, to reach which he had made a wide aerial detour. He had decided this, lest the bridge should have been destroyed: also, there was the possibility, if not the probability, that by landing on the far side he might have laid himself open to discovery by some band of Kebreau's men moving down to join the others. The fact that he had been able to land without the Heinkel showing up suggested that the latter was not in the vicinity, or if it was, that it did not go up for a very good reason: the rebels required to preserve the secrecy of their movements. It might even be that the Moth had not been seen or heard. Even if it had, there would be those amongst Kebreau's men who would know the railway surveyor made occasional flights in the ordinary way of his work. Because the machine had not made any attempt to investigate the scene on the bridge, it was fair for Rapson to assume that the rebels might think they had not been observed.

"We're having to take a chance, that's all," he told Fawden, easily. "We'll pack a couple of the hand bombs each in case we run into trouble. We'll also have our revolvers."

"And ruddy cheek!" Fawden grinned.

Rapson frowned at him. "If you'd rather not——" he began, but Fawden shook his head vigorously.

"I'm not funking, sir!" he said. "But it struck me sort of comical for a couple of fellers to go against —well, we don't know how many of 'em there are!"

Rapson laughed. "Don't worry," he said. "I'm not intending to do anything so darned silly as to attack! My idea is to try to find out where the rebels concentrate and then bring back a bunch of our fellows—if it's possible, that is."

"You're the boss, sir," Fawden admitted. He weighed one of the bombs in his hand. "Haven't held one these since I was demobbed. It was a Jerry hand-grenade which gave me the only Blighty I got. Yes, I'm ready!"

They set off across the open stretch of country, plunged into the surrounding jungle, climbed a hill and descended into the forest-filled valley beyond. Rapson took course by his compass, and after a while reached the river bank. As they travelled, the pair of them blazed trail by notching tree trunks with their bush-knives.

"There's the bridge!" said Rapson at last. "It's intact! Must mean that we were either not seen or, if so, my stunt of keeping off worked. But we'll go easy, Fawden, in case anybody's been left behind."

It was a case of almost wriggling through the forest now, in order to keep under cover, but presently they saw the clear trail made by many men. There was an old trail leading from the bridge through the hills, but it was littered with oddments thrown away by marching men. It was an easy trail to follow, and it took them five miles, twisting and turning through the forest, showing here and there signs of where short halts had apparently been made. Rapson, in front, held up his hand as his keen ears caught sounds ahead.

"Maybe they've made another halt," he whispered. "Or perhaps they've camped for the day. After all, the attack doesn't take place until to-morrow night. I should reckon we're about twenty miles from camp. They wouldn't be likely to risk camping nearer than that, I think. Twenty miles wouldn't take many hours and as they've probably got native guides who could lead them in the dark, they could start just before sundown and get in under cover of night. Off trail now, so that we can approach safely."

They succeeded in doing this, guided by the scent of fires. They found themselves looking out on to a natural clearing, surrounded by trees which met in a thick canopy overhead. It was an ideal spot for a camp. A hundred aeroplanes could wing over and see nothing. Here and there were fires, with men sitting and lying around them. They were set well away from a big pile in the centre of the clearing. Rapson saw that this was made up of rifles together with boxes undoubtedly containing ammunition. Ted made a hasty calculation and decided that there were several hundred men in the clearing, at one side of which, set apart, was a tent. Through the opening of it he saw three men—Liberians all of them; and one he recognized.

"George Washington!" he murmured, with a smile

at the incongruous name for a Negro. Incongruous, yes, but after all, the Liberians were descendants of American Negroes. Washington had been in the Government Department administered by Kebreau before the "purge". On a box in the middle of the tent were a bottle or two. Mr. Washington and his companion-officers evidently did themselves well. They were arguing over something, but owing to the hubbub of voices, Rapson could hear nothing.

"Listen!" he whispered into Fawden's ear. "I'm going to sneak round to try to hear what's happening. If I get into trouble, I'm going to chuck my bombs at that ammunition dump—you do the same, and then make a bunk. If the luck holds, we'll meet at the 'plane."

"Okay, sir!" said Fawden. "What you say goes!"

And Ted Rapson left him and began a somewhat unpleasant journey round the clearing, aware that at any moment he might either stumble into a Liberian or a lynx-eyed Negro might spot movements amongst the trees and give the alarm.

"Which," Rapson grated, "would be darned unfortunate for a lot of people, I reckon!" He was holding one of his bombs, ready to pull out the pin, and to send the thing hurtling towards that heap of explosive stuff in the centre of the camp.

CHAPTER X

JUNGLE WAR

THE rebels were too busy to bother about possible intruders: they were eating. Yet Rapson was very cautious as he went, because sentries might have been posted. When, however, he did not see any, he decided that George Washington's army did not think there was necessity for them. The aeroplane could not have meant anything. If Kebreau had contacted with Washington after the affair down at the railway, he had probably given it as his opinion that the cause of it was simply the reappearance of the Heinkel, and that the delivery of the message to Lingard was unknown.

One thing which intrigued Rapson just now was whether one of the two men with Washington was or was not Kebreau: Ted had been unable to see the faces of the two. It was largely to settle this point that he had decided to risk trying to get near to the tent, which he accomplished at last without his presence being discovered.

He lay in the undergrowth behind the tent. A matter of five yards or so was between him and it. He cautiously looked about and considered that he ought to be able to reach the tent without being seen: everyone was engaged, eating, drinking, talking—arguing, as explosive sounds now and then suggested.

"I'll chance it!" he gritted and wormed along the ground, his heart in his mouth. He went flat at the tent, waited a moment or so, and then eased up the bottom of the canvas and got his ear to the opening thus made.

It took him some time for his ear to become accustomed to things so that he could pick out a word here and there; and when he succeeded in doing so, he licked his dry lips. Neither of the men in the tent was Kebreau, whose name was mentioned several times. Piecing together the words he caught, Rapson was able to make a coherent story out of them. George Washington, a little bit drunk, had decided that he was not going to wait until the next night to make an attack on the railway camp. He was going to make it this very evening. He intended to start in another hour or so, after the men had rested. It seemed they had marched a long way: Rapson gathered that they had obtained arms smuggled across the frontier from Sierra Leone.

Washington's companions were his subordinates, but they tried to dissuade him from anticipating Kebreau's orders.

"If anything goes wrong," Rapson understood one of them to say, "I wouldn't like to be you."

"Don't worry!" Washington boasted. "We'll raid that camp and have the train and the arms and ammunition there. Plenty of dynamite, too, which will come in handy. I'll bet Kebreau will make me Vice-President!" He laughed drunkenly as he said this.

"If you mess things up," the other said, "Kebreau'll make vulture meat of you!"

So the argument went on, but nothing further developed; Washington had made up his drunken mind. Rapson eased his way back into the undergrowth, where he could lie safely while he considered matters. The problem was whether four bombs pitched amongst that ammunition would do sufficient damage to prevent Washington's force from going down to the camp. There would be no time, apparently, for Rapson to get back to his machine and come back with the intention of plastering the place with bombs and machine-guns; even if there was, he realized that he could not possibly locate the clearing.

"Whatever's to be done, must be done right here!" he murmured. "Unless I fly back to camp with the alarm. But there are too darned many of the rebels for us to stand a chance against them. They've got machine-guns as well as rifles. Somebody's likely to get it in the neck in Sierra Leone, I hope! Well, what?"

For a long while he lay there, trying to formulate a plan, or, rather, trying to make up his mind whether it would be possible to set off the ammunition dump —and make a getaway. The latter was as important as the former, because possession of the Moth was likely to prove valuable to the defenders of the railway against Kebreau's own attack.

Long trailing lianas, hanging down from the trees, gave Rapson an idea.

"Yes, that might be a way of evading discovery!" he decided. "But I ought to let Fawden know so that he gets a good chance, too—I'll go round and see him!"

He made the return journey as cautiously and as safely as he had made the previous trip. Fawden did not hear his approach.

"Strewth!" Fawden mouthed, when Rapson's head showed close by. "If you'd been a Lib. you could have shot me."

"I was scared stiff I might make a sound and that you'd plug me!" Rapson confessed, softly. "Listen, Fawden!"

For the next few moments, Rapson spoke quietly, telling Fawden what he intended to do, and added: "You'll wait in the tree until things quieten down. So shall I. Then you'll pick up our back trail, and we'll meet at the river—I hope! If we rout the rebels they're almost certain to head for the river and cross it. So it'll be a case of our moving through the forest, keeping the trail in sight until we reach the river. Then we go back on our blazed trail to the Moth—and here's something darned important."

"Looks like everything's darned important, sir." said Fawden. "If anything happens to you, I can't fly a blessed 'plane!"

"That's what I'm coming to," said Rapson. "If you get there first, take out some of the bombs. Don't disturb the camouflage. Make a bunch of scrub of yourself by getting underneath some branches near enough for you to chuck your bombs if by any chance some of the rebels show up. The machine mustn't fall into their hands. Blow it to hades—and I hope you'll be able to get away!"

"Hu-uh!" Fawden breathed. "Okay, sir!"

"You're a good scout," Rapson commended. "If

H

I get to the 'plane first and the rebels show up, things'll have to be a bit different. We need the machine." He paused, but Fawden did not show signs of alarm. "If I do reach it first," Rapson went on, "I shall get rid of the camouflage and have the engine warming up—ready for you. But in the event of rebels turning up I'll have to take off alone. Do you mind having to take the risk of staying around, keeping hidden, of course, until I can come back and land if everything's clear—I'd bomb the rebels, of course, to make things clear?"

"Go ahead, sir!" came from Fawden. "I was once the only survivor in a pill-box and just had to stay put until some of our blokes retook the position."

"Yes, you're a good scout!" Ted assured him. "Well, you know what to do, and when! I'm off!"

He made his way back to the rear of the tent. He went just as cautiously as before, despite a diversion created by a sudden mix-up on the part of some of the rebels. Rapson knew nothing of the cause, nor cared. He did know that Washington and his two companions came drunkenly out of their tent and, by using revolvers, settled, in blood, the argument, whatever it was about.

That diversion, which kept Washington away from his tent for a while, enabled Rapson to shin up one of the lianas to make sure that it would hold his weight later on. He had not intended making this experiment, but to take his chance when the time came, but the ructions in camp suggested the possibility of the safe, precautionary measure.

Satisfied, he slid down to the ground, and went to cover.

Presently, he knew that the three officers were back in the tent. But for the fact that during the row a milling crowd of rebels had been between him and the dump, he would have acted at that time. But he had to wait for comparative quiet. When it came, he was ready. He stood up behind a tree, drew the pin from one of his bombs, which he sent hurtling across the clearing. As it left his hand, he took the pin out of the second bomb and as the first fell on the dump and exploded, the second was on its way. So was the first that was thrown by Fawden.

Pandemonium broke lose. The exploding bombs set off ammunition in a series as though made by gigantic Chinese crackers. The rebels were flung into confusion—many of them were killed by erupting bullets which looked like a pyrotechnic display—and scores more died when, suddenly, the whole dump went up in a terrific roar. Rapson, who had shinned up the liana and taken refuge amongst the leafy branches of the tree, realized that there had been bombs in that dump. He also realized something else.

At the first explosions, Washington and his companions had run out of the tent, but had jumped back for its meagre shelter as the bullets began to fly. When the big explosion happened, the blast from it uprooted the tent which flopped down on top of the three officers. A moment later, two of them went wriggling from beneath its folds of torn canvas, but Mr. Washington was not one of them. Ted saw them running into the forest, whither the majority of the rebels had already gone. Smoke filled the clearing. Already, some of the fringing trees had taken fire.

"Wonder," grated Rapson, "whether Washington's dead?"

He slid down his liana, determined to find out. He dropped to earth, ran to the wrecked tent, knowing that if any of the rebels saw him, they would not know him for a white man: he had smeared his face, while in the tree, with muck off the liana and leaves. He believed he would be taken for some mad fool of a rebel who was risking his life from still-exploding cartridges, to rescue George Washington!

Rapson tore away the canvas, and saw Washington lying there, on his back. His black face looked horrible. Blood was wet on it, and his thick red lips were darker than nature had painted them. Rapson knelt beside him, felt over his heart, knew that the man was alive.

"God! I've got to secure him somehow!" Rapson gritted. "After this dies down some of 'em may come back to look for him!"

He dragged the unconscious Liberian away from the spot, to the foot of the tree, tied the loose end of the liana around him, beneath his armpits, and then he himself shinned up the rope made by Nature as strong, almost, as any made by man. On the stout branch above, Rapson straddled, and began to haul up the unconscious man. It was slow work, for Mr. Washington was no lightweight, but at last, somehow, Rapson got him on to the branch, between himself and the trunk of the tree. He shoved him along it, down into the crotch, and lashed him securely to the branch. Then he gagged him, sliced his bush-knife through a liana, and bound Washington's arms.

All this time—and it had not taken very long—new fires were breaking out, and rebels were scurrying away from them. That Rapson had not been observed was not surprising, since some of the rebels, filled with the lust for loot even in that grim setting, had fallen on the food stores, fought amongst themselves for possession, and men died with knives in their hearts—while the forest was blazing.

The crackling of burning foliage was like the sound of heavy rifle-fire. A breeze, blowing from east to west, fanned the flames—and Ted Rapson thanked the fates that his tree-refuge was on the east of the clearing. But he remembered Fawden, away there to the west!

"Let's hope he bunked immediately he'd chucked his two bombs!" Rapson murmured, as screaming natives went crashing through the undergrowth beneath him. Even the looters were going now, joining in the stampede to the east.

"They won't stop running for miles!" Rapson thought. "And they're going right away from where we left the Moth!"

But although the fire was sweeping westwards, the heat was terrific, even where Rapson was perched in the tree. He would have to go down presently, for flying sparks had ignited some trees not far away from him. The Moth had been left to the south-west and unless the wind changed, that way would be safe for travelling—after the fire had burnt itself out around the clearing. Rapson knew it had spread for a long distance. He was by no means in good shape. His eyes smarted, his mouth was dry, his whole body tingled as if it had been pricked with red-hot needles. He coughed until his throat ached as though it were being cut with a blunt knife.

"I'm going down!" he choked presently. "I'll make east for a bit, then detour!"

He unlashed Washington, who was still unconscious, and lowered him to the ground. He slithered down the liana after him. Men were screaming in the clearing, men who had been wounded during the explosions. But Rapson could do nothing for them. Through the smoke he saw some of them crawling. Others were lying still—very still. He somehow hefted Washington on to his back, and went stumbling with him into the undergrowth, tramped by the feet of hundreds of fleeing men. He tripped over a fallen man, who clawed at him, but missed. Rapson went on—on—and on. He halted for rest, all too frequently after a time. But he braced himself to the effort again and again, and presently decided that he was far enough away to risk a longish stay before beginning to work his way round.

Even at this great distance, the air was hot. Smelt hot, and of smoke. Afar off, there was a crimson glow, which now and then was blotted out by a black pall of smoke. Animals of many kinds crashed through the jungle and none of them heeded Rapson; they were all too scared of the flaming horror to take notice of man. Birds squawked high up, and monkeys screamed as they swung themselves through the tree-tops.

"God only knows whether I'll be able to get through!" Rapson gasped as he took up his burden again.

There were miles to go to reach the Moth, and part of the distance must be down the trail by which he had come up from the river; and it ran through the fire-area. Would he be able to find it, was the problem that confronted him. He had only his compass to guide him, and his experience of the trail had told him that its twisting, indeterminate character might lead anywhere. But he held on. He reached a smoking area, and knew that he could not cross it.

"Not for hours!" he croaked, as he put Washington down. They were several hundred yards from the smoke, but the tang of it surrounded them. The fire was raging miles ahead of them. Rapson found something compensatory in it all.

"Line's going to run through here! Fire'll save us plenty of work. Hello, so you're round, are you?" He had set Washington against a tree trunk, and the Liberian's eyes had opened. Long since Ted had taken the gag out of the man's mouth; he could do no harm however loudly he might shout. Washington had received a wound in the chest and another on his head.

"Who—are—you?" he asked, and seemed to have difficulty in focusing his eyes.

"The name," said Ted, "is Rapson, Mr. Washington. Or is it to General or Colonel?"

Washington seemed to be swallowing something. For a moment or two he did not speak. He threw glances about. Then eyed Rapson strangely.

"Looking for the rest of us?" Ted asked, with a grin that hurt his taut skin. "There were only two of us."

"Liar!" Mr. Washington spat the word, and then winced at the pain the effort produced.

"I forgive you, Colonel," said Ted, cheerfully. "It was really the fact that you had your ammunition in one dump which enabled us to do the impossible. Looks as though you won't be able to do even what you thought was possible, doesn't it. You won't be able to disobey Kebreau's orders, will you?"

"I know you," said Mr. Washington. "You're the surveyor. But what do you know of Kebreau's orders?"

"Thanks," Rapson grinned.

"What for?" Washington demanded. He moved, as if he wanted to stand up. But he found it difficult, owing to his arms being bound. He relaxed. "Why thank me?"

"For telling me that a gentleman named Lingard hasn't met you since yesterday," said Rapson, easily. "Although he didn't know what was in it, he'd have guessed, when he met you, that the letter probably contained something about—about that!" Rapson waved a hand, as if to embrace a lot of things. "You see, Colonel—you are a Colonel, at least, aren't you?" he asked, as if it was important for him to know the standing of his prisoner.

"You go to hell!" said Mr. Washington.

"Not yet, I hope," Rapson chuckled, and wished he had not, owing to the pain in his throat. "You were supposed to attack our camp to-morrow night,

but had decided—you were drunk, I know—that
you'd do it to-night. Well, you won't be able to,
will you?"

"My men will——"

Rapson interrupted Washington. "Your men can't
do much. They're mostly without weapons, I imagine,
and the way they were running when I last saw them—
those, that is, who could run—I reckon they're well
on the way to wherever they came from."

"Shut up!" Mr. Washington was not polite.

"I thought perhaps talking would help pass the
time," said Ted, "until we can resume the journey to
my aeroplane."

Mr. Washington blinked, as if he remembered
something.

"I suppose you thought we were on a survey,"
Rapson grinned. "You did see us, eh?"

Mr. Washington once again consigned Rapson to
a place reputedly hotter than the jungle that was
burning in the east.

"Well, I don't blame you for not admitting you
made a mistake," Ted said. "By the way, I'm sorry
I haven't been able to do anything about your wounds.
But I haven't got a kit. When—that is, if—we get
to the 'plane, I'll patch you up. How do you
feel?"

"As if I'm burning up inside!" Mr. Washington
told him.

A man can afford to spare sympathy for a wounded
enemy. "I'm sorry," Rapson admitted. "By the
way, do you happen to know where Kebreau is?"

Somewhat casually, as he asked the question, he

pulled out his revolver. Washington laughed, hoarsely, painfully.

"If I knew, I wouldn't tell you," he said. "And that's just bluff on your part. You'd never shoot a wounded and unarmed man!"

"All right, you win, Colonel!" Rapson grinned.

CHAPTER XI

TRAITOR'S "LUCK"

"You know, Washington, I think you've got guts!"
Ted Rapson spoke in a quiet, sincere tone. Hours
had passed since he and his captive had first talked
together. Some of those hours had been spent in just
sitting down to wait until it would become possible
to travel. When they had decided to do so, they
found conditions by no means easy. They made a
detour which took them well away from the burnt-
out area, yet even so, changes of wind brought smoke
bearing down on them, together with clouds of ashes.
They were soon like walking scarecrows. They had
spoken but little, owing to thirst, for they had found
no water. Washington, despite his wounds, had
behaved splendidly: a man of endurance, was Rapson's
decision regarding him.

Washington drew a dry tongue over cracked lips.
"What else could I have done?" he asked. "If I
hadn't kept on I'd——" He hesitated and looked at
Rapson with bloodshot eyes. "It's just the same,"
he resumed, "whether I gave up in there," he waved
a hand back towards the jungle they had left some
time ago, "or go to face a firing squad when you
hand me over."

"It is a bit of a devil, isn't it?" Rapson murmured.
"But we'll think about that when we get to camp.

Let's get to the top of this hill, so that I can see if my machine's still there."

From the summit of the hill, he looked down on the plain where he had landed. There was the Moth.

"Yes, it's okay," he said, but Washington stared uncomprehendingly. "Oh, I forgot," Rapson grinned. "The 'plane's hidden under that mess of branches."

"Why didn't you come over and bomb us?" Washington asked.

Rapson explained the impossibility of finding the rebels from the air, and added: "Besides which, I wondered whether Kebreau was there. If he was, I wanted to get close up on the chance of grabbing him. Instead, all I got was you. Let's go down. There's something to eat and drink in the 'plane."

That thought served to whip up the flagging spirits and remains of Washington's strength. The two men, white and black, although the grime on Rapson successfully concealed the colour of his skin, hurried down the hillside. Ted was wondering if Fawden was there. The fact that there was no sign of him did not worry Rapson a great deal, because it was the obvious thing for Fawden to remain hidden until he was assured of the identity of the newcomers. There was, of course, another possibility, which Rapson did not overlook. Fugitive rebels might have discovered the machine. If so, they might have decided to leave it intact on the chance that its owner, who, they would realize, must have been responsible for the surprise attack in the clearing, would come back. It was a risk which had to be taken. Rapson would have been unable to approach the camouflaged 'plane unseen, except by night. Darkness would soon be on them, and Rapson could not wait for it, because he must take off while there was daylight.

Boldness, therefore, was required, and presently Rapson gave a hail. He thought, or at least meant it to be, a loud one, but his voice was cracked.

"Ahoy, Fawden!" he shouted. "This is——"

He had no need to finish Fawden came out from cover of the second pile of branches, set at about fifty yards from the camouflaged machine. Actually, Rapson had forgotten all about that, or its presence would have set his mind at rest immediately he saw it.

Fawden came hurrying towards them.

"Get back and start on the branches!" Rapson called, knowing that time was precious. When he and Washington reached the Moth, Fawden had torn away much of the camouflage. Rapson climbed up and started the engine. He came out again with food and something to drink. Washington, squatting on the ground, choked as the spirit burnt his parched throat.

"Now let's patch up that shoulder and head," Rapson said. "Finished, Fawden? Good fellow. If you don't mind, I'd like you to doctor Colonel Washington—it is, Colonel, isn't it?" he grinned at the Liberian. "I'm sorry!" he exclaimed, as he saw Washington's face. "That's darned mean of me. Hurry up, Fawden! You look horribly fresh compared with what we do. How'd you get on?"

"Tell you presently, sir," said Fawden, who climbed up into the machine. He returned with the first-aid kit, and while cleaning and padding Washington's wounds, told Rapson that immediately he had flung his two bombs, he started to run. When he realized the fact of the fire, he was on the trail down to the river, and kept going full pelt, reached the river, tore across the bridge, and when on the other bank, cut the bridge down.

"The fire was behind me all the way," he said. "But I'd got a bit of a start and managed to keep it. I worked my way along the river bank, swam across after a while, and reached here some hours ago. I made sure you'd lost out, boss!"

George Washington gave a queer kind of a grunt. "Two men who'd have the blasted cheek to do what you've done, couldn't lose out any time."

Fawden chuckled. "Why," he asked Rapson, "didn't you try to make that trail?"

"I was on the wrong side of the camp, for one thing," Ted told him. "If I'd tried to cross it or go round I'd have been seen and that would have been the last long trail for me! Besides which, Mr. Washington was lying under the wreckage of his tent and I wanted to find out, if possible, whether he was alive. He was. So I decided to take him up into a tree with me. There I had to stay, and when I did get down, it was impossible to reach the trail. So we went a long way round to get here, and I'm telling you, Fawden, I feel nearly all in. What Mr. Washington feels like I can imagine. So when you've finished with him——"

"Five more minutes, sir," said Fawden: and within ten minutes the three men were tucked into the Moth which went streaking across the plain for the take-off.

It was possible, before night fell, to look down and see the vast area over which the fire had spread.

"Pretty thorough, eh?" Rapson called over his shoulder.

"Washington can't talk, sir," he heard Fawden yell. "He's just been sick and I reckon he's fainted."

Rapson did not answer. He was giving all attention now to flying the Moth. He gave the engine the gun, without flying very high: he believed that he would be able to get over camp before the sharp night fell. If so, that would make a landing easy—and Dave Dawson would not be worried regarding the identity of the machine. Rapson did not fancy a landing in the darkness—and he felt there would be a decided reluctance on Dawson's part to have flares lighted on the landing-field without knowing whether the 'plane was the Moth or Kebreau's Heinkel!

Luck held. The Moth behaved well, and Rapson sailed over railhead while the sun was still over the horizon. Men were down there in a big crowd. Rapson saw something go streaking along the line, and knew it to be a hand-trolley.

"Dave going to meet us!" he grinned; and a few moments later throttled down, and was going in a glide towards the landing-field. He made a thistle-down landing—and he and his two companions were walking towards the line when Dawson came running up from it in the sudden darkness.

"My God, Ted!" Dawson raved. "Where've you been? We saw a forest fire——"

"Which," said Rapson, "Fawden and I started!

It was later, when they were all in Rapson's room, that, with a good meal under his belt, he said:

"Sorry I set about you, Mr. Rapson. After all, you saved my life. Now, can I ask what you're going to do with me?"

"Just hold you until—until later," Rapson told him. "It means, of course, you'll have to be under guard all the time, and won't even be allowed to move around camp."

"Fortune of war!" Washington admitted. "I wanted that food—now I want sleep."

The doctor had attended to his wounds, which were not serious, except that they had caused him to lose much blood. Now he was taken to an office opening out of Rapson's. In it, a couple of cots had been put, and Chalmers was given the job of sleeping in the same room, as guard.

When the prisoner had been disposed of, Dawson asked Rapson: "What do you think, Ted? That Washington's men realized it was an attack, or would they believe something had exploded in the dump?"

"If they're all like Washington," Ted grinned, "they'll think the latter's the explanation. He told me he and the two officers with him thought so at the first crack. Afterwards, there wasn't much time for anybody to try to understand what had caused the show. Anyway, I suggest we go ahead just as if nothing had happened."

"Regarding Kebreau and the supply train?" Dawson asked and Ted nodded.

"Yes, we'll get some men down the line at daybreak, and have them in hiding, ready to tear up a

I

section of the line just before nightfall. Nowhere near a village, of course. As a matter of fact, I've thought of a good spot. It's near one of my early landing-fields. I'm going to take the 'plane down there so that I shall be all set if Kebreau turns up with the Heinkel, which isn't unlikely."

"I reckon his idea is," said Dawson, "to get the trains, load 'em with his men, and then have them driven right into Monrovia. They'd be able to do that, where they wouldn't find it easy to march in. If things were to go off up here as they want them to, they could reach Monrovia at daybreak. Our station's right near the government buildings, which they could probably rush before it was known they'd arrived!"

"It's a bet, too," said Rapson, "that Kebreau's got men under cover in the town, waiting for him. If anything goes wrong at our end, we've got to get word down to Monrovia in time to warn the Government. Perhaps, indeed, we're doing wrong by not telling them right away, but, really, I think if we can scotch Kebreau's plan up here, we'll perhaps save bloodshed. There'll be no rising in Monrovia if he doesn't turn up."

"Well, we've made a good beginning!" Dawson laughed. "We'd better forget things and get some sleep now, I reckon. What? Of course! I've set four men on to guard the Moth—two on and two off during the night."

Ted Rapson needed no second suggestion about bed. Nor did he need rocking when he flopped down on to his pillow.

But it was not an undisturbed sleep.

He was awakened by a revolver shot. He sprang out of bed and rushed to the door leading into the room where Chalmers and Washington were. He barged in and almost fell over two men fighting madly on the floor. He could not see them and he darted back into his own room, found a box of matches and a moment later struck one in Chalmers's room. He saw Chalmers on his back, with another man on top of him. Chalmers was doing his utmost to force up the man's hand which held a revolver. On the bed lay Washington, unable to move because he was bound hand and foot. A shot rang out, and the bullet whistled past Rapson's head. He flung himself to the floor as a second shot came through the opened window.

He heard the shouts of many men outside, and the sounds of a scuffle. He got to his feet and risked another light, saw Chalmers's opponent drive a fist in under his chin and Chalmers relax his grip on the fellow's arm. Next moment the man's hand dropped and a bullet would have ploughed into Chalmers's face if Ted had not lashed out his bare foot. It took the fellow on the elbow—and the contact nearly broke Ted's toes. But it sent the revolver flying from the man's hand and then Ted was at him. He flung one arm round the fellow's neck and hauled him off Chalmers. Ted's other fist pounded into the man's kidneys and made him yell.

Dave Dawson came bursting into the room, followed by several other men. A lamp was lighted, and Ted saw that the newcomers had brought in a man who looked as though he had been half killed.

"Found the swine outside, Ted!" snapped Dawson. "Saw him pump a shot in through the window. He's Lennards and—so you're another of 'em, eh, Morris?" He glared at the man who had been attacking Chalmers.

"They're the fellows, I've no doubt," said Rapson, "who turned Lingard loose! What happened?" he asked Chalmers.

"The window was open, of course," the latter answered. "I was awake and saw someone at it. Didn't do anything or say a word, but just waited for him to come in. Thought I'd have a better chance with him inside. When he was in he stood to one side of the window and then suddenly let fly at me. Guess he must've seen the light patch that was my face. Missed me, though, and then I fired at him, but also missed. We mixed it, then, and I reckon he'd have got me if you hadn't come in, sir!"

"Tie 'em both up!" Ted ordered. "Dave, we're going to keep watch until morning!"

"Okay," Dave nodded. In Ted's room, he added: "Trouble is, we don't know whether there are any more of those fellows. In the morning we may find that one or two are missing—gone to tell Kebreau things."

"None have been missing!" Rapson said. "If Morris and Lennards knew where to find Kebreau they'd no doubt have left with Lingard. Odds are that neither they nor Lingard knew where Kebreau could be found. They waited here, while Lingard skipped, in case they might be useful. Anyhow, we've got 'em—whereas to-morrow we should have taken them down with us and they'd have had an opportunity, or tried to make one, to warn Kebreau!"

"That," Dawson grinned, "is one way of looking at it!"

CHAPTER XII

HOLOCAUST

THE spot chosen by Rapson at which to intercept, if fortune were kind, the supply train, was about ten miles from railhead. Because he was in ignorance of how many, if any, of his men were in Kebreau's pay, but felt certain some were, he knew it was useless to try to put up a bluff as to why he was taking an armed force out.

"It's a case of chancing everything," he told Dawson. "We'll take the men down in the train, which we'll send back. I'm going to break the news to them and see how they take it."

The white workers took it in good fashion. Some of the Liberians did not appear to be so enthusiastic, and Ted put matters on a volunteering basis as far as they were concerned. The result was that he found himself with a little army of several hundred men.

So, much later than Rapson had originally intended to leave—having to come out into the open regarding his plans meant there was no need to send men out in apparent working-parties—he stood and watched the entraining of as strange an army as ever even Africa had seen. Black men and white climbed into the trucks, and Rapson got aboard with them. He was going down to set men at work clearing the landing-field of some of the new growth which, he knew, must be there after months of disuse. He was intending to return by the train and then fly the Moth down and have it waiting in case of emergency. It now carried a second machine-gun, in the front cockpit; Rapson did not intend to be caught napping as he had been when tackling Kebreau a couple of days before.

The train disembarked the army at the appointed spot, and Rapson led off a large party of the men to the adjacent landing-field. As he had expected, it was over-run with new growth, but the brawny workers set to with a will to make a clearance.

"They'll get it done before evening," he told Dawson. "I'll go back by the train and come in later on the Moth."

He climbed aboard the train, and, arrived at railhead, was told that, judging by telegrams from Monrovia, nothing was yet known there about the impending attack on the train. When, later on, he left in the Moth, Rapson was carrying a telegraph-linesman's set, with which to tap the wire should it become necessary to get in touch either with railhead or Monrovia.

He set the 'plane down at the cleared landing-field, without seeing anything of his army. But Dawson presently appeared out of the fringing jungle.

"No, I didn't see anything which would have aroused suspicion," Rapson grinned in reply to Dawson's question. "We'll keep n the jungle until it's time to sling the sleepers across the track. Perhaps we'd better camouflage my machine in case Kebreau should take it into his head to make a reconnaissance flight—which I really don't expect him to. But that's why I wouldn't have the line blocked yet—he'd be able to spot the obstruction if he came on in advance, and then fly back and give the alarm."

But Kebreau did not put in an appearance, and the remaining hours of daylight passed, night fell with its usual directness, and Rapson had the camouflage taken off his machine: the search-light, sweeping along the track as a warning to straying animals, would not pick out the 'plane where it stood a quarter of a mile or so away from the line. The men hidden in the jungle came out and took up positions nearer to the track, under cover of the thick scrub: the machine-gunners found ideal "nests" behind some of it. The men were on either side of the track, and in the clearing where the Moth stood, Rapson had had piles of dry, tindery scrub placed at safe distances. They were designed, if need should arise, to provide him with light by which to take off. The machine was turned into the light wind that was blowing, and the engine had been allowed to turn over for some time, so that it should be warmed up, ready to taxi away.

There was still a long wait ahead, even after darkness, as Rapson knew. If the train travelled without being held up, it could not reach the position chosen for the proposed ambush for several hours yet. The track stretched into the night in a straight line: Rapson had selected the position because it would be possible to see the approaching train while it was yet a long distance off.

He saw the haze of its searchlight, then the glaring eye of the latter, long before he heard the train itself.

When he did hear it, he knew there was something significant in the sound.

"Not running smoothly," he murmured to Dawson. "Suggests there's an inexperienced fireman at work! Hardy would never fire an engine like that, Dave! Get ready, boys!"

He shouted the order into the darkness, and received answers from the unseen, waiting men, tense, every one of them, wondering what was to happen. When it did happen, it found them ready.

The train rattled into view, its searchlight streaking along the line ahead of it, and presently picking out the sleeper-obstruction on the track. Not a man moved yet, however, obeying orders.

"Is it going to stop?" Rapson wondered. "Or will the driver only slow down and try to force the sleepers off?"

The train stopped, about fifty yards from the obstruction. A man jumped down from the footplate and in the glare of the searchlight, Rapson recognised him: it was Richardson, regular driver of the train. He ran up the line, reached the obstruction, stayed but a few moments, and then raced back to his engine, bawling for helpers.

Immediately, a number of men leapt to the ground, and Ted Rapson knew that the train had been taken: he knew how many men should have been on the train, and those who jumped down were more than the complement. He waited until they reached the obstruction: it meant splitting up the defenders of the train. Then he blew shrilly on the whistle he carried, the agreed-on signal for action.

Shots rang out from the concealed men, and several of those struggling with the sleepers crashed to earth. Instantly, from the trucks firing began and bullets whanged into the darkness which had been split by rifle and revolver fire. Someone in the scrub quite close to the track lobbed a grenade over and there followed a terrific explosion: Rapson realized that the bomb must have dropped into a truck loaded with dynamite.

Out of the other trucks shouting men tumbled, as if they were afraid of other explosions and felt that they would be safer fighting in the open. But not all the rebels sprang out: some, working machine-guns, stayed where they were, and the darkness was broken by their stabbing orange flames. The bombed truck, containing as it did, other stores, was now in a blaze. Ted, sighting along his rifle, tried to pick off one of the machine-gunners, but the job was done for him by one of his men slinging over a bomb.

Railroaders went down beneath the hot fire of the rebels, but their comrades carried on. The rebels were between the two parties of Rapson's force, one on each side of the track. On the other hand, the rebels were also in two sections, each of which had the protection of the train against double attack.

Rapson's machine-guns chattered in answer to those of the rebels. Bombs were thrown by both sides, but the rebels, unable, against vicious firing, to reach the cover of the scrub, were forced to hug the train's sides, and the railroadmen were able to plaster them with bullets and shift their own positions into new cover whenever they wished. Some of the rebels, realizing that in their scare they had made a mistake by jumping out, began to clamber back into the trucks, but Rapson's men prevented the majority from doing so.

The train could not be driven backwards, because the explosion of the dynamite had wrecked the coach and torn up the rails, blown a great hole in the track. It was a case of fighting it out—and blazing, barking, chattering weapons made the night hideous, while screams of men told of attackers and defenders suffering agonies.

"The darn thing'll soon be alight from end to end!" Rapson mouthed, as two trucks caught fire. Men from them scrambled into others. A flung bomb dropped into another truck and set off some cases of ammunition.

Above the uproar of shouting, screaming voices, cracking guns, exploding cartridges, bursting of an occasional bomb and the blasting of dynamite, Ted heard a yell, someone calling him.

"Who is it?" he bellowed back, and then the rattle of firing drowned the other man, if he replied. Presently, Ted heard him again.

"Caught a feller telegraphing!" the man yelled. "I——" His voice rose to a crescendo of agony. Rapson called, but got no answer.

"Reckon a bullet found him, Ted," said Dave.

"I'm going up in the Moth!" Rapson told him. "I imagine the fellow who was telegraphing was trying to get in touch, if he hadn't done so already, with Kebreau. It's a likely thing, y'know, that he'd be waiting somewhere down the line, probably for word that the train was nearing railhead. Then he'd fly up to take part in the fighting there, if necessary. Means these men had a linesman's set, and Kebreau another."

"Maybe you're right, Ted," Dawson commented. "If so, it'ud be as well for you to be up."

As Rapson turned to worm his way through the scrub, another of the trucks caught fire, and the defenders, caught by blasting bombs as they tried for other shelter, decided to make a break from the train. They swarmed out of the trucks—all except two men who sat in one, working a machine-gun for all they were worth at the flashes of flame which came from the attackers.

Dawson crawled through the scrub, with bullets snarling all about him. He sprang from cover presently and went streaking towards the train, got close enough and sent a bomb hurtling through the air. The machine-gun's chatter was swamped by the crash of the explosion as Dawson turned and scurried back into cover.

"That's put done to them!" he panted, flinging himself down.

Men were beating it down the track. Bullets sped after them, as, wisely, the railwaymen remained under cover. Dawson heard the roar of an engine, knew that Rapson was taxi-ing across the clearing, looked away to the right and saw the Moth climbing.

The light of the blazing trucks flashed on the 'plane's wings. It also showed Rapson the men fleeing down the track, and he presently banked to come over the line.

"No, dammit, I can't!" he grated. "Can't machine-gun them. They put up a good fight and if they can get away, let 'em! This ought to be the end of Kebreau's little game, I think!"

But Fawden, who had been waiting at the machine, suddenly tripped the toggle of his gun, and Rapson jerked back so sharply that he pulled the stick and the Moth's tail went down.

"Shut up!" he roared over his shoulder, as he put the machine's nose down, righted, and then, banking away, came into the straight again and began to climb.

"Thought we were going to blast 'em, sir!" Fawden shouted.

"So did I—but I couldn't, after all!" Rapson threw back at him. "Would have been very nearly like murder. Maybe I'm a fool, but there it is, Fawden! We're going to climb and fly around about here in case Kebreau comes up."

"Okay, sir," said Fawden, who realized the wisdom of Rapson's plan. By remaining near the spot where the train was burning, they might be able to find Kebreau's 'plane more easily, if they were high enough. A machine could not pass over that line of fire without being silhouetted and seen by someone in another flying above. If Kebreau had received intimation of what was happening, and he had the Heinkel with him, he would certainly not waste any time. All depended on how far he was away. Rapson had his tanks filled with petrol and could remain in the air for a considerable time.

Down below, he could see the pin-points which he knew were flashes made by firing weapons. Set like a flashing jewel in a dark velvet frame, was the burning train.

"There's likely to be an unholy row about that," he murmured, "until folk see sense. They'll say I ought to have warned Monrovia and prevented the business from happening, but I think I've done the right thing. True, we've lost some men—I hope not too many. But there'd probably have been worse trouble if the Government had acted down on the coast."

Now and then he throttled down his engine, to give him a chance to listen for the sound of another 'plane. Time and again he did it, without hearing anything. But there came at last the rip-roaring sound of an engine fully opened out; and it was so comparatively close that he was alarmed that the other 'plane might have gone beneath him without being seen. He opened out again, and began to circle round so that he came above the fired train. He remained there, like a kite wheeling preparatory for swooping after its prey. But Rapson could not see the other machine yet. Once or twice he throttled down again, but could not locate the direction of the other machine.

"Keep your eyes skinned, Fawden!" he shouted.

"Righto, sir!" Fawden said, and it was Fawden who spotted the silhouetted Heinkel down below. He almost screamed the information to Rapson who now succeeded in making out the shadow above the blaze.

Then, suddenly, it was gone—and he marked the pyrotechnic display which he knew was coming from the red-hot exhaust of the Heinkel. He saw, too, orange flashes, and knew them to be flames from machine-guns, firing down, blindly, he hoped, at the scrub-covered earth. But suddenly, the Heinkel turned—its exhaust seemed like a giant catherine wheel.

"It's climbing!" he grated. "Bet we've been spotted!"

He knew that the Moth's exhaust was just as visible to anyone observing, as was the Heinkel's, which became more vivid. Rapson guessed that the Heinkel was flying full speed forward, and a few moments later realized that it was zooming: the fireworks were being ejected in a downward burst.

"Ready?" he yelled at Fawden, and pushed the stick forward. The Moth went into a power-dive, and its two machine-guns blazed as it went. From the Heinkel, as it zoomed, gun-flashes leapt. Whoever was piloting it, did not mean to let his opponent have it all his own way. Rapson pulled the Moth out of its dive, banked and went round, to come behind the Heinkel as it flattened out. The Moth's guns sprayed the Heinkel from tail to nose, and Rapson almost screamed as he saw a flame lick along the machine, and then as he kicked rudder to bank and turn away after passing the other machine, he almost screamed again. There was no resistance to his kick—something had gone wrong. He drove his other foot down, but still there was no response. The only explanation could be that the tail had been shot away.

The Moth was at a good height, and was headed in the direction of the railway. Rapson wondered whether he could make a landing, but even as he wondered, the machine slipped off.

"Bail out, Fawden!" he roared over his shoulder. "Remember——"

"I won't forget!" came from Fawden. "What about you?" He was already climbing out on to the wing.

"I'm going too!" Rapson yelled. "Hurry, for God's sake!"

Fawden shot off the wing. Rapson could only hope that the plucky chap would remember the instructions about the use of the parachute. Rapson himself followed a second or two later, flinging off as far as he could. The Moth slid down, rather went down in a spiral as Rapson spotted the bellying parachute of Fawden.

If it had been physically possible for him to scream at that moment Rapson must have done so. But all he could do was to forget his own counting and to stare with horror-filled eyes at Fawden swinging right under the falling 'plane; and then, Fawden was blotted out—and Rapson did not see him again. The machine had struck him, his parachute was caught, tangled, ripped.

Rapson pulled his cord automatically. His speed of drop eased up and then he was floating.

"Oh, my God!" he panted now.

He was floating above a world of fire. Down on the line the train was blazing. Away to one side the forest was on fire, ignited by the fallen Heinkel. There were other lights, too: tiny flashes which Rapson realized were being made by rifles and machine guns.

HE WAS FLOATING ABOVE A WORLD OF FIRE

Facing page 144.

Inferno—into which he was descending.

"No, by God, I'm not!" he grated as he discovered that the light wind was carrying him northwards. He had leapt from the Moth when it was a great distance from where he had seen those first flames licking about the Heinkel. If he were lucky he should land well away from the forest fire and be able to escape before the wind blew the flames farther—unless he were caught in the jungle top.

Right across the railway the wind took him; he knew it because the fire seemed to slide past him. He also knew that he was safe to the extent that he would be on the side away from the jungle conflagration when he landed, and the cleared stretch of land through which the railway ran would stop the fire in that direction.

There was, however, no hope of his landing on terra firma: that much he knew. He travelled a good distance over a dark world now, for the blaze was far behind him. That luck could hold and put him down in a clearing he did not believe: he was not the man to build false hopes. He felt something touch his feet—drew them up instinctively, but he went lower and found himself entangled amongst tree-tops. The parachute tugged at him. The trees tugged too. Rapson waved his arms. Better to grasp the trees than to be dragged amongst them, perhaps strangled by severed cords of the parachute. The 'chute defeated the tugging trees, he was swept farther, then dropped into space, was hauled up again, and floundered into a tree. Rapson swept his arms about the foliage which seemed to consist of stabbing spears. He clung desperately, heard the ripping of the parachute which had carried him safely and now seemed to be regretting it.

Rapson twisted his legs amongst the foliage and so held on with hands and feet. The tension eased after a while, and he guessed that the parachute, torn into a score of pieces, probably, had been caught and held.

"Safe, so far," he gasped.

CHAPTER XIII

AFTERMATH

RAPSON succeeded in extricating himself from his parachute harness by cutting it, and without tumbling down from his leafy perch. Up there, he could see in the great distance the jungle fire. He reckoned he was about a mile from the railway. He succeeded in striking a match by which he consulted his compass.

"Guess I can find my way," he muttered as he set about making down the tree. That tree was all of seventy feet in height, and Rapson did not clamber down the last twenty feet. He dropped. There was nothing else for it. He could not get his arms around the trunk, which was now bare of branches. He landed amongst undergrowth, fairly shaken, but unhurt, as he discovered when, presently, he was able to stand up.

Finding his way by compass reading was comparatively easy: but the way itself was difficult for he had to tear a path through the thick undergrowth. He stumbled and crashed. Sharp thorns tore his clothes to ribbons. Birds and animals, disturbed by his thrashing, squawked and squealed and made for safety from the unseen terror by night. But Rapson went on—on until at last he broke from the jungle and saw the full awesome beauty of the distant fire. Thwarted by the cleared country the fire had extended lengthwise—and Rapson saw, silhouetted against it, the dark bulk of what he knew was a train. It was not the one that had come up from Monrovia, but one which, as Rapson knew, must have been telegraphed for to railhead. Tiny figures of men flitted about against the background of fire, but they were too small for him to make out what they were doing.

He stumbled on his way, limbs aching, his body burning from innumerable scratches; and he was an exhausted man when at last he sprawled to the ground through stumbling over an inert body not far from the line. He lay there for a while, regaining his breath. Then he fumbled with stiff fingers and discovered that the man near him was dead. Rapson clambered to his feet, tried to shout, but only a croak issued from his throat. Presently he was near some men and realized that they were carrying a stretcher towards the train. He managed to attract their attention and they put down their burden.

"Say, who's that?" one of them asked.

Ted grated out his name, and the two men came running towards him, caught him as he fell forward; and when he awakened, he was lying in a rocking truck and could hear the sounds of a labouring engine, which told him the train was climbing one of the many steep gradients. Stars gleamed above in a dark velvet sky. Men were talking around him. Others, not so near, were singing. Rapson sat up and the man squatting next to him jerked round.

"How do, Ted?" It was Dave Dawson who asked the question, and struck a match as he did so. Ted blinked at the light which went out suddenly.

"Feel as if I've been thrashed all over, Dave!" he said. "What's happened? I mean since——"

"Not a lot, Ted," was the answer. "Have a swig of this," and he handed Rapson a flask. "When I found you were alive, Ted, I just let you sleep. There wasn't anything you could have done, anyway. The fight was over and we were picking up the wounded."

Rapson handed back the flask. "Many killed, Dave? On our side, I mean?"

"Eight," was the quiet reply. "About thirty wounded. There were, as far as we've been able to discover, sixty of Kebreau's men killed and a few more than that wounded. Probably their casualty list is higher, though: the dynamite explosion may have accounted for a lot more. By the way, it tore up both sets of metal, which is why we're going to railhead instead of down to Monrovia as I'd hoped to be able to do so that the wounded could get proper attention. We've got 'em on the train.

"Fawden—you saw him, Dave?" Rapson asked, quietly.

"Poor devil—yes," Dave said, and gripped Rapson's arm. "I—I didn't know it was he until—until I saw you, Ted. What happened? The machine crashed into the jungle. It's burnt up, of course!"

Rapson explained and told, briefly, the story of the short combat with the Heinkel.

"Did you see anybody bail out of it?" he asked, eagerly.

"No!" Dawson said. "I saw the 'plane was on fire, but it was too far off to see anything else. You were nearer when you had to bail out, y'know. Trying to make a landing, of course. I asked some of the men whether they'd seen anything, but none had."

"What I'm wondering about," murmured Rapson, "is whether Kebreau was in the Heinkel. Oh, I know he said in the letter that he'd be waiting down the line with the Heinkel. But all kinds of things might have happened so that he wouldn't be in it. What about some of his men? Take any prisoners—wounded, for instance?"

"Yes, we've got his wounded on board with our own," Dawson admitted. "But we've been too durn busy to question them. We'll do that when we arrive."

In due course, railhead was reached. Doctor Colling had gone down in the train to attend the most urgent cases. Now he enlisted volunteer aid and set to work in real earnest, while Rapson and Dawson tackled the less seriously injured amongst the prisoners. But none of them could say whether Kebreau had been in the Heinkel: or if they could, would not.

"Leaves us in the dark, Dave," Rapson said. "What about Monrovia, by the way? Did you telegraph after the rebels scattered?"

"Tried to!" was the gruff answer. "But the line was dead. Reckon it had been cut south of the fighting. Couldn't send down to find the place, because the rebel fugitives would've sniped our men. Gad, Ted, but we've got a heap of work waiting for us to-morrow down there!"

"We, or I, rather," Rapson smiled grimly, "have also got some explaining to do! There's Darcy, for one. He'll be sure to blow up because I tackled this on my own responsibility. And what the President will say, I can't imagine!"

"Huh-huh!" growled Dawson. "I know what he should durn well say: Thanks! Come along with me!"

"Where?" Rapson exclaimed.

"I'll show you!" snapped Dawson, and took him to the doctor's hut. "Give Rapson a look over, Doc!" Dave said. "He was beginning to take off the rags he's wearing ready for a wash. He's scratched and torn so that his body looks like the lay-out for a jig-saw puzzle."

The Doctor gave a cursory glance at Rapson's body.

"Strip," he ordered. "Lord knows, but in this climate any of those wounds might turn septic."

He cleansed the wounds, sterilized them, and when he had done, Rapson, looking at himself in a shaving mirror which he shifted occasionally, grinned.

"Jig-saw, eh, Dave?" he asked. "Right now I look like a patch-work quilt, with all these strips of plaster!"

"Better to be a patch-work quilt than a corpse," Dawson assured him.

"Reckon so," Rapson agreed. "I'm going to turn in, Dave. Will you warn the men who stayed up here that they're going down early to repair the line? The men who fought had better have a breather. I mean," he grinned, "the rank and file. I want to be called to go down."

He went back to his own place.

Morning. The camp was a-buzz when Rapson came out. An engine was all ready. In trucks scores of men were waiting. New rails were gleaming in the sunlight as they lay on trucks.

"Say, Dave," Rapson found Dawson checking up requirements. "Have a hand-trolley put on board. If we can't locate the break in the telegraph I intend to travel down to Monrovia by the trolley. If we can, however, I'll get Darcy to send up an engine. I've got to go down and face the music."

"Ought to be a couple of brass bands to greet you," Dawson grinned. "Okay, Ted!"

Presently the train pulled out. On instructions, it went slowly, in case, during the night, the line had been tampered with. A heavily loaded hand-trolley was in front of the engine which pushed it forward. The weighty thing rattled down the line, and Ted reckoned it would be sufficient to set off any mine which might have been laid. Time and again the train fetched up with the trolley, and sent it speeding ahead. Nothing, however, happened, and the scene of the fighting was at last reached.

One side of the line was virgin jungle. The other was a blackened vista from which smoke still issued here and there.

"My God!" exclaimed Rapson, when he came to examine the scene. "That hole's big enough to swallow a couple of engines! It'll take days to fill it in!"

"Reckon so," Dawson agreed. "But—er—Ted!" He waved a hand. "Those poor devils have got to be buried somewhere!"

"Yes!" Rapson nodded, understandingly. "Better have them searched—maybe there are papers on some of them which will prove useful to the Government.

Also things which can be handed over to relatives—
if the Government agrees. First thing to be done is
to send down to find the break in the telegraph."

Two hand-trolleys were derailed and man-hauled
to the other side of the broken line. Here they were
put back on the rail. The front one was loaded with
twisted rails and fish-plates. It was ahead of the one
on which the linesman and his assistants were to
travel. The first was again to act as a "pilot" to
test the safety of the line. Driving it ahead called
for hard work on the part of the natives who worked
the levers, but it was a necessary safety precaution.

Rapson was busy superintending the reconstruction
work, after the great hole had received its grim packing
of dead men, when a messenger came up to him.

"Henley reports, sir," the man said, "that he's
found the break. Will you come over?"

Rapson hurried over to where a linesman had tapped
the wire to be ready to receive any message which
Henley, in charge of the break-down gang, might
send through. Lewis, the linesman, handed him a
paper on which he had transcribed a message. It
was from Henley.

"Soon after repairing line," it ran, "got a message from
head office. Darcy says has sent out gang to find break.
I told him I had found it, but did not say what had happened, acting on instructions."

Rapson slipped the paper into a pocket.

"Get head office for me," he ordered, and Lewis
began to work his portable transmitter.

"Through, sir!" he looked up presently, and

Rapson sat down in Lewis's place. He could telegraph and he proceeded to tell Mr. Darcy what had happened during the night—and before. Darcy interrupted now and then to ask a question. At the end, Rapson sent:

"I want to come down to report. Can you send an engine for me? If not, I'll use a hand-trolley—though God help the men who'd have to handle it."

"I'll send an engine at once!" Darcy promised. "I'll get in touch with the President and ask for troops to go with it in case of trouble."

"Okay!" was Rapson's laconic answer to that, and went back to his work. Darcy had been reasonable. He had asked why Rapson had not given his information to Monrovia. When Ted had told him why, Darcy had said nothing more than: "Well, the Government have the last word. We're covered—if the Government keeps its promise. If you can, get the prisoners down so that they can be brought here."

Hours later, an engine, pulling a couple of trucks, filled with armed Liberians, drew up near the scene of the fighting, now the scene of sweating labour. Rapson had sent his own engine back to railhead; and the wounded rebels had been brought down. They were put on the newly arrived train. With them were the more seriously wounded workers. Captain Jefferson, who was in charge of the train, sat in a guard's van, now at the front of the train as it was being pushed back. With him was Rapson, who had left Dawson in charge of the working party.

"I got a bit of the story, Mr. Rapson," Jefferson said. "But not all." He puffed smoke, and waited.

"You got it that this was a Kebreau affair, then?" Rapson asked, and the Captain nodded.

"Seeing him," he said, indicating George Washington, in a corner of the van, "would be enough to suggest Kebreau! We've got a long run ahead, and the yarn ought to help it pass."

"All right," Rapson grinned, and told of the events since his reading of the letter which Kebreau had delivered to Lingard.

Mr. Darcy, who had come with the train from Monrovia, and who was also in the van, answered the question with which Rapson ended his story.

"Yes, you did right, Ted!" he said. "I saw the President and told him what you'd given me. He took it well, and says that the Government will keep its word to us in every respect."

"Fine—I feel all right now!" said Rapson.

"I suppose there hasn't been time to do anything about looking for the Heinkel?" Jefferson asked.

"No time at all," Rapson assured him. "Why?"

"Thought perhaps it might be possible to say whether it had anyone in it when it crashed and burnt," was the answer. "Kebreau, you know."

"The Heinkel fell on to the jungle," Rapson reminded him. "I doubt whether it would be possible to say how many men might have been in the machine: the heat of the forest fire would have been simply tremendous—and the odds against finding the wreckage are hundreds to one, I imagine."

"So we'll be in the dark about Scarface Kebreau!" said Jefferson. "And won't know whether he's alive and due to break out again some time!"

That was the chief burden of President Coolidge's wail when, in due course, Rapson had made his personal report before the hastily convened Ministerial body.

"You and the men under you, Mr. Rapson, have done a great thing for Liberia!" the President said. "We understand why you decided to deal with the situation as you did and appreciate the fact that you believed by doing so you might prevent a considerable rising with dreadful loss of life here, in Monrovia. The Government have decided to implement the agreement entered into when the Railway Defence Force was organized. Compensation will be paid for damage and personal injuries, and, also, of course, to relatives of those unfortunately killed. But—but against what you succeeded in doing there remains the fact that, had you given us your information, it might have been possible for us to have secured Kebreau. Time will have to show us whether he escaped."

"Sorry I couldn't bring him in, sir," said Rapson, simply. "Perhaps Washington or others of the prisoners may give valuable information, from which you may learn where Kebreau's secret headquarters are. Or were—he'd probably change them if he's escaped."

"You can leave Washington and the others to us, Mr. Rapson!" said the President, harshly.

"Certainly, Your Excellency!" Rapson tapped his fingers lightly on the arm of his chair. "By the way, sir, although I quite understand that the matter of compensation is bound to take a certain length of

time, there is one thing I'd like replaced as quickly
as possible."

President Coolidge glanced sharply at him,
inquiringly.

"The Moth, sir," Rapson said. "The fire beyond
railhead means that it will be necessary to make an
entirely new survey up there and——"

"Quite—I understand." The President turned to
Darcy. "You are empowered to negotiate for the
purchase of a new machine."

"Thank you, sir!" Rapson got up, and a few
minutes later was making towards the company's
offices with Darcy. "Better cable home about the
Moth," Ted said. "Ask for quick delivery—they'll
send it out by boat. Sooner we get it the
better."

"H'm," came from Darcy. "We've got to get some
new trucks, too, Ted. I'd hoped to be able to have
the line working up to railhead, but the President
says no. He declares that we ought to wait to see
whether all the trouble's over."

"Maybe he's right at that," Rapson suggested.
"If Kebreau did escape, he'll be a very angry rebel!
It would be a pretty rotten start if any of the earliest
trains we ran were blown up, wouldn't it?"

"God, yes!" Darcy agreed. "I reckon Kebreau would
be capable of doing that. Not everybody in Liberia
has been or is in favour of railways and those who
aren't would probably gloat over disaster."

Rapson chuckled.

"You remind me," he said, "of what I've read
about the beginning of railways in England! Mass

meetings of protest, and ministers preaching against the idea. In England, remember!"

"I know, I know," said Darcy. "I also remember when we had to have a man walking in front of us when we first used motor-cars. But you can't stop progress, Ted. Nothing can."

CHAPTER XIV

NO. 1437

"EVERYTHING'S fine, Dave." Ted Rapson was back at railhead, after his visit to Monrovia. Dawson was back, too, the work down the line having been finished. "We even succeeded in getting the Government to extend the time-limit set for us to push the line up to Binoh."

"Unless you'd done that, Ted," Dawson assured him, "we'd have been behind time, which would have cost a pretty penny under the penalty clause."

"Long before we reach Binoh my new machine 'll be delivered," Rapson told him. "Then I can make the new survey over the burnt area. Meanwhile, the Government's going to be busy having a clean-up. Troops were sent out while I was in town to round up the fugitive rebels down the line. Those higher up probably scattered to the four winds. Anyway, they haven't a leader, unless Kebreau escaped, which is doubtful. Opinion in Monrovia is that even if he escaped, he's probably finished."

"On the principle that a fellow who fails so certainly, won't be hailed, even by discontents?"

"Even Liberians haven't quite shaken off the shackles of tabooism," said Rapson, with a slow smile. "It's in their blood, Dave. It's deeper down in the natives of the country, from whom Kebreau has been recruiting. Anyhow, the Government believes that the sequence of failures by Kebreau may make the people think he's taboo, unlucky, and all that sort of thing."

"Let's hope so," Dawson grinned. "My bet is that Kebreau's finished—finished and dead. And if he's not dead he's a washout."

The uncertainty regarding Kebreau's fate remained, but as time went on, there seemed little doubt about another important matter. From reports received from Monrovia, Rapson learned that mass demonstrations of loyalty to the Government were held all over the country, and large numbers of rebels, betrayed by weaker brethren, were arrested. Some of them had been with the small army commanded by George Washington, and troops, brought to railhead by train, marched and swooped on the rebels in little villages. Significantly enough, nothing was heard of Kebreau, and it was assumed that he had met his fate when the Heinkel fell in flames.

Meanwhile, the line was being pushed forward. Rapson, waiting for his new 'plane, found plenty to do in the way of surveying. Jim Leader was recovered from his wounds and the labourers had settled down to their work beneath the sweltering sun.

It was Jim Leader who brought Rapson a message one afternoon.

"There you are, sir!" Leader said, handing him a paper. "Just come through from Darcy."

Rapson took the paper and read what was written on it.

"Great!" he exclaimed. "Boat's due on the 9th

and I'm going down on the 10th to pick up the new Moth. We'll soon be busy taking new photographs, Jim!"

"Suits me," Leader grinned. "I'll admit I've missed the flips we used to take. They kind of bucked a fellow up, after having been grounded in this heat."

Leader was not more pleased than Rapson himself, who during the next day or so felt a growing impatience, as he worked, to be on the way down to Monrovia. But there was no necessity to go before the boat arrived, and he carried on.

There had been no further trouble as far as the railway work was concerned, and he had come to think that there would be none. Disillusionment, however, came on the morning when he stood, almost hidden by the jungle, on the bank of a river, turning the thumbscrews of his theodolite, and looking through its telescope, trying to get his "line" across the river. Near him was his gun-bearer, a native named Gogera.

The slowly moving telescope stopped. Rapson's brows wrinkled as he looked through the glass. While, thanks to the jungle, he was as he realized, almost invisible to anyone on the opposite bank. On the other hand, his telescope, bringing the bank close up to him, enabled him to see things quite clearly. What he was looking at now was a man, clambering backwards down the high bank. He was clad in the loose trousers of the railroad native labourers, and on his right arm was an armlet, bearing his number: 1437.

"What's he doing there?" Rapson muttered. Ted knew that none of the workers should be near the river. Railhead was two miles away on the native's

L

side of the river. Rapson had crossed in a canoe to verify the survey he had taken from the opposite bank.

As Rapson watched, and wondered, the native came to a halt some distance down the bank. He dug in his feet, stood poised precariously for a few moments; and Rapson saw him take something from his trousers pocket and put it into a hole in the bank.

A moment later, the man was climbing back the way he had come. Ted was on the point of hailing him, then decided not to so do, but to look into the hole. He remembered that previous message which had been delivered to Lingard—and remembered what had followed.

"Good God," he grated. "Does this mean we've been living in a fool's paradise?"

He kept his telescope trained on 1437—and gasped as the man grabbed the top of the bank. It was not the man's action which caused Rapson's concern.

"A leopard!" Ted exclaimed. In his glass, he saw the spotted brute emerge from the jungle growth, nose crinkled as if sniffing. Then 1437 had his head above the edge of the bank—and hung there for one brief second, staring into the eyes of the leopard. Then, with a yell, he let go, flung himself backwards and turned a somersault in mid-air as the leopard sprang for him.

Ted Rapson jumped from his theodolite and almost knocked Gogera over. He snatched the sporting rifle from the boy's hand, jumped to the edge of the bank, as 1437 and the leopard crashed into the river. The native struck out wildly. The leopard, swimming like a dog, went after him, Rapson threw his rifle to his shoulder, drew a bead on the animal, and fired.

Crash!

The echoes rang through the jungle, drowned a second later by the roar of the leopard.

Rapson knew he had found his target, yet the animal was still swimming. Ted shot at it again, and saw a new and growing patch of reddening water. The leopard lashed wildly; he was wounded but not done. Rapson slipped another cartridge into his double-barrelled gun and let the leopard have it.

"That's finished him off!" he snapped. He cupped his hands and bawled: "Come here, 1437! It's all right now!"

The native, who had thrown but one hasty glance behind at the first shot, now looked round again, trod water, stared up at Rapson for a moment or so, and then struck out madly down river—away from where Ted was standing.

"Well!" Rapson exclaimed. "I save the blighter's life and then he does a bunk. Why?"

The action of the native, following his mysterious business at the hole in the bank, served to increase Rapson's concern.

"Wait here, Gogera!" he rapped. "Watch where the leopard comes up—I want his skin!" Then he was scrambling down the bank to where the canoe lay, hidden by sweeping trees. He climbed in, pushed off, and went paddling merrily in the wake of 1437.

The native threw a scared glance over his shoulder, saw the canoe chasing him, and promptly made for the bank whence Rapson had come. He beat Ted to it in good style, and with plenty of time to spare, thanks to his start: and Ted had the annoying vision of the fellow clambering up the bank.

"Stop or I'll shoot!" Rapson bellowed, but he knew he would not do anything of the kind. Probably the native also knew that, for he did not stop. He went climbing up and up, reached the top as Rapson pulled in his paddles and made a show with his revolver. The native waggled cheeky fingers at his nose, and then dived into the jungle.

Rapson grinned to himself. He could have dropped the fellow without unduly injuring him, but reckoned that by doing so he might be going further than circumstances justified. Also, he could get from the hole whatever the native had put into it.

Rapson started back up river, and stopped when he spotted the body of the leopard. Using the canoe deftly, he eased the animal into the bank opposite where his theodolite was standing, and presently had it roped to a tree. While he had been doing this, Rapson had been thinking. No. 1437 had been afraid of him, probably because he thought Rapson had seen him at the hole. Rapson wondered whether the native would lurk about and watch what he did.

"If I don't go near the hole," Ted muttered, "he'll think I didn't see what he was up to. There must be something mighty funny afoot for the blighter to bunk after my shooting the leopard off him!"

So Rapson paddled back to where Gogera awaited him, and went on with his surveying job, finished it, and then crossed the river to help Gogera get the leopard up to the top of the bank. They used ropes over tree branches in place of block-and-tackle, and Rapson chose the position for the job. He selected the point where the hole was into which 1437 had slipped his "something".

With Gogera on the bank, hauling at the leopard, Rapson climbed up with it and steadied it, so as to avoid spoiling the skin by tearing it, as might have been the case if it had been caught by the numerous protruding roots. The work meant stopping very often—and once Rapson stopped at the hole. It was the work of a second for him to slip a hand in, under cover of the lepoard, and then he had a hidden envelope in his pocket.

"Tie down, Gogera!" he shouted. "I'll come up and do some hauling now." He did not spare his lungs. If 1437 was on the other bank, he would be bound to hear the shout. A few minutes later, Rapson was behind the tree over a branch of which the leopard-laden rope was thrown, and lashed to the trunk.

"When you're ready!" he called to Gogera, who was going down to where the animal was hanging. But Gogera was not yet there, and Rapson examined the envelope. It was crinkled and dirty. It carried no address. He slipped a pencil under the flap and rolled it carefully, so getting the flap open without tearing it or the envelope itself. A few moments more, and he had read the writing on the paper which he drew out. Gogera yelled at this moment and Rapson returned the letter to the envelope which he slipped back into his pocket. Then he began to haul away at the leopard, which at last they got on to the bank. Afterwards, they drew the canoe up—and during this little job Rapson, who had come to a quick decision, licked the envelope, smoothed down the flap, and then slipped the letter back into the hole in the bank.

On the bank, Rapson and Gogera set about the work of skinning the leopard.

"By heaven!" Rapson murmured as he worked. "More trouble—and this lot's aimed directly at me! Tchk!" The exclamation came as the result of a near-cutting of his finger as his knife slipped. "I'd better pay attention to this job!" he grunted. "Thinking can come later!"

CHAPTER XV

THE ABYSS

SITTING in his office, Rapson had reached the point of telling about his discovery and reading of the note which the native had hidden in the hole in the river bank.

"Well, what did it say?" Dawson asked, anxiously. "Is it Kebreau again?"

"I don't know that," Rapson admitted. "It didn't say. What it did say wasn't much but plenty." He broke off. "I reckon this is what I've been looking for." While talking, he had been searching through a lot of papers, chits, requisition forms and so forth. "I thought," he added, "I recognized the writing as some I'd seen before. It was written by Vic Blakey!"

"But what did it say?" Dawson cried.

"Just this," Rapson answered. "I didn't have time to copy it, but I can remember:

'R. goes down on 10th to fetch machine. Special coach. R. driving. Hold up at Mugualla Hills. R., who will deliver your note, will put up show, but it will be faked. Dozen or so workmen on train but they won't worry you.'

"There was no signature," Rapson said. "But it's a fortune to a fish-plate that the letter was written by Blakey. Fairly clear, isn't it?"

"Meaning, what?" Dawson asked. "Oh, I know

that R. stands for Richardson, who's driving the train."

Rapson smiled. "There's nothing important being taken down and the letter, unlike that one we got from Lingard, makes no mention of armed men. Just mentions—er—me."

There was a frown on Dawson's face. "You think it's an attempt to get at you, Ted?" he asked.

"Can think of nothing else," Rapson admitted. "If Kebreau's alive, he may consider he's a very good reason for having a personal smack at me, Dave. Those few words about R. delivering the note suggest to me that when I've been dealt with the train will be allowed to go on. Where are you going?" Dawson had suddenly got to his feet and turned towards the door.

"Going to stick a gun into Richardson's ribs and bring him in here!" was the quick answer.

"Sit down, Dave!" Rapson smiled. "I want to talk some more."

Dawson obeyed.

"You see," Rapson went on, "I couldn't stay or even leave Gogera to watch that hole in order to find out who'd collect the letter. 1437 could hide in the jungle and keep watch—probably did. He'd find a way to warn whoever came for the letter. The odds are that it would be a native—and he'd be no darn use to us, would he? I left the letter purposely because I intend to let things take their course, Dave!"

Dawson put a light to his pipe. "You've had the devil's own luck so far, Ted. But, will it hold? God! I'd like to get Richardson in here and put him through the mill to make him talk! And Blakey, too, the swine!"

"I know, I know," murmured Rapson. "But they wouldn't talk. Don't forget that Richardson was driving the train which Kebreau's crowd held up. We couldn't get anything out of him except that he just had to pull up and his fireman was shot. Now, of course, we know that he was in the tricky game."

"So you think it's Kebreau again?" Dawson asked

"Who else—except Lingard?" Rapson countered. "I don't think Alf Lingard would have all that much interest in me. After all, he was only a paid hireling of Kebreau. By letting things take their course, Dave, we ought to be able to find out whether this is a Kebreau affair or not. But that's got to wait until I get to Mugualla Hills!"

"I think——" Dawson began, but was interrupted.

"That I'm goofy, eh? Well, Dave, they say that forewarned is forearmed. In two days' time I'll know the answer. Meanwhile, it will be just as well to keep tabs on Blakey."

"I'll see to him!" growled Dawson, but although he kept his word, he saw nothing suspicious about Vic Blakey. Look out was kept for 1437, but as was to be expected, he did not put in an appearance; and on the 10th, Ted Rapson boarded the construction train, bound for Monrovia. He was the sole occupant of the special coach attached to it, right behind the engine. Richardson was the driver, and he had a big negro for fireman. If all went well, according to schedule, the train would enter the Mugualla Hills at nine o'clock at night. Long before then, Richardson had turned on the searchlight that was necessary for safe travelling, but Ted had turned off the light in his compartment. He did not, however, go to sleep.

Actually, he was riding the buffers between his coach and the engine when the brakes went shrieking on. Here and there along the train, the natives who had been brought along in case anything was wrong on the newly laid track, set up a hullabaloo, of which Rapson took no notice. He heard someone drop to the track from the engine, then Richardson's voice yelling—as the door of the coach behind crashed open. Footsteps were on both sides of the coach. Richardson was demanding of someone:

"What's all this about? Who——"

"Keep your hands up!" another voice answered him—and Ted recognized it.

"Lingard!" he gritted. "By God, what——" A revolver barked, and Lingard yelled "Grab him!" Rapson smiled grimly to himself as he straddled the buffer. "Richardson putting up his show, I reckon!"

A scuffle followed, above which Richardson's voice shouted, cursed; then died away.

And meanwhile, something seemed to be happening in the coach. Ted had seen lights of torches on both sides of the coach, and someone was saying:

"He isn't there! I'll swear no one opened the door before she stopped!"

"Same here!" came another voice, from a man on the footboard on the other side. "But where has he gone? Ask Richardson."

The speaker's voice had a harsh accent to it. Rapson did not remember having heard it before.

"Yes, Mr. Rapson came with us!" It was Richardson speaking now. "But what the devil——"

"Shut up, you!" Lingard mouthed at him. "Hey, everybody!" Voices, many voices, shouted back at him. "Get busy—look in every truck and find him!" Rapson knew that the hold-up gang consisted mostly of natives: their voices told him that.

"A little disappointed," he murmured. "Can't make out if Kebreau's here! Perhaps it's just a little matter of Lingard's personal——"

Even his thoughts were interrupted by the crack of several revolvers and the yelling of many voices on both sides of the track. Rapson dropped from the buffers now. He knew what was happening. A band of labourers, chosen for proved loyalty, had been sent out the previous night, unknown to Richardson and Blakey. They were in the charge of four whites, and they had travelled by hand-trolleys and, reaching the Hills, had lain hidden, waiting. Now they were in action—and so was Ted Rapson.

He emerged from between engine and coach in time to see a man drop from the latter, shouting wild orders to wraith-like figures which were dashing all over the place. These were, as Rapson made out, natives. He pumped a revolver shot at the jumping man, drilled him through the shoulder, and sent him crashing amongst the group around Richardson. The white near Richardson threw up a gun and snapped a shot at Ted, who ducked as it came. Then Ted was in, smashing his gun-barrel into the face of Richardson, and knocking him completely out.

The next moment, Rapson found himself wrapped

in a rare tangle with the man who had fired at him.
It was Alf Lingard.

"You treacherous swine!" Rapson panted out the
words as they fought—the while that a scrap was
going on in many different spots. Naked natives were
fighting with the railway negroes and whites, but
Rapson had not much time to think about them.
He was having a stiff time with Lingard. Each had
the other's gun gripped, each had a hand clasped
about the other's throat. Lingard kneed Rapson in
the groin and nearly won the fight right then. But
Ted managed to hold on to him. Suddenly, however,
Ted let go of Lingard's throat and pounded several
terrific jolts to his chin, finishing up with a thunderous
blow to the body which sent Lingard sagging away.
He let go of Rapson's wrist, and Ted stumbled forward
from the impetus of his own blow. As he tried to regain
balance, a hand gripped his ankle, jerked it, and he
crashed to the ground. He hit his chin heavily, but
that was the least of his troubles, for something struck
him a terrific whack on the back of the head and
after a momentary blaze of flashing lights, Ted Rapson
faded away into an abyss of darkness.

When he came to, he was in a canoe; and the sun
was flaming down on him.

Black-skinned natives were paddling rhythmically
in front of him. Sounds told him that others were
paddling behind him. For a few moments he lay
where he was in the bottom of the canoe. The natives
were chanting as they wielded the long paddles, and
Rapson realized that there were canoes before and
behind the one that carried him. Suddenly a man

spoke from the stern of Rapson's canoe. It was the voice with the harsh accent.

"How's Schwartz now?" the man asked, and a voice from the front answered:

"Reckon he'll cash in, Woolf!" It was Lingard speaking now.

"A pity, Lingard," Woolf said. "Rapson? Oh, he's still out. He must have got a nasty whack when the nigger hit him. Another couple of hours and we'll be in camp. If Schwartz lives until then we may be able to save him."

Then silence again, except for the swish of water as the paddles were worked. But every so often, Woolf and Lingard talked—and Rapson kept still and quiet. He wanted to learn things, if possible.

He did learn some things, too: he discovered the explanation of his being in that canoe, and it was not a pleasant explanation. The fight had gone completely against the railroad workers, largely because the attackers were in greater numbers. Two of the whites sent down from railhead had been killed, and the two others wounded, whereupon the negro labourers had fled. Richardson had been made to fight on the side of the attackers—and had been killed.

"Richardson can't blab, as he might have done," said Woolf. "Blakey'll probably make a bolt when he hears."

"We still don't know why those niggers were sent down," said Lingard. "1437 told us that nobody went to the hole after he put the letter in. He was sure Rapson didn't. The nigger was watching all the time Rapson worked at the leopard."

"Himmel!" came from Schwartz. "Rapson's as cunning as a fox. He must have seen 1437—that's why he hauled the leopard up right near the hole! But what's that matter? We've got Rapson and Kebreau'll be glad to see him. Haw-haw!"

Kebreau! The one name that Rapson had been waiting to hear. So Kebreau was involved—and this was no petty affair of personal revenge on Lingard's part! It was much worse than that, seemingly: revenge on Kebreau's part—and Rapson did not feel at all comfortable as he thought about it. The Liberian, who had been twice foiled by Rapson, was not likely to use kid-glove methods.

"I said trouble, and by heavens, I was right!" he muttered. "But I'm still wondering what Kebreau's going to do!"

He found out, partly, when at last he was yanked out of the canoe, admittedly conscious now, and carried to a camp some distance from the river.

Vicious-eyed, cruel-mouthed, scar-faced, Kebreau was squatting on an upturned box in the little clearing into which Rapson was taken.

"Good!" Kebreau scrubbed his pale-palmed hands together. "You got him! The charming surveyor who interferes with other people's plans!"

Natives came in, carrying Schwartz, who, however, died in a few minutes: he had been shot through the chest.

Rapson stood in front of the smiling Kebreau, hands tied behind his back.

"So you escaped!" Ted said. "And like a rat went into hiding! You don't look much like a future

President, Kebreau! And nearly naked natives don't make me think you'll ever be one!"

Kebreau got off his box and before Ted realized what was going to happen, drew a hand across his face. Rapson laughed.

"Grown childish?" he asked, smoothly. "If you want to use your hands, give me the use of mine and I'll show you something!"

"Show me something!" Kebreau's voice was hoarse. He winced as if with pain, lifted his topee and Rapson saw that his head was completely bald. Not only so: there was a shining metal plate over part of the bare skull. Kebreau saw Rapson's eyes on it.

"Yes!" he snarled. "I came down by parachute that night, but half my head was torn away by something as I landed. I got away and—— My God, Rapson! You're going to pay for all you've done!"

"I can take my medicine!" Rapson retorted. "I hope better than some men can! May I ask what you're going to do with me?"

Kebreau dropped back on to his box.

"Hold you to ransom!" he said, harshly. "We're asking twenty thousand pounds and your new machine for you, Rapson!"

Ted looked at him as if the man was mad.

"I'm not worth it, Kebreau!" he said, simply. "Also, I don't think anyone else will believe I am. Who do you think is going to pay? I suppose that's what was meant by 'R. will deliver your note'?"

"So you did find the letter?" jerked Kebreau. "I thought you had. Well, it doesn't matter now." He looked over at Lingard. "What about that note?"

"Richardson was killed," Lingard answered. "But I'd given him the ransom note before that and it 'ud be found on him."

"Good!" Kebreau exhibited no concern over Richardson's fate. "I reckon," he rapped at Ted, "that your company will be willing to pay twenty thousand pounds for you and throw in the 'plane! Why? Because if they don't, they'll waste time! They'll need a new surveyor—they'll have to face constant wrecking of the line and—you've got a penalty clause in your contract, haven't you?"

Rapson breathed deeply.

"That line'll never go through if the money isn't paid!" snarled Kebreau. "I want money now—money, do you hear?"

"For another attempt at a rising?" Rapson asked, musingly, almost as if to himself.

"Damn the rising!" shouted Kebreau. "It's money I want. I'm going to clear out of Liberia. I can't get out in the ordinary way. The ports are watched here and in Sierra Leone and the Ivory Coast. But if I can get a 'plane——" He shrugged his shoulders as though his meaning must be evident.

"Supposing the company doesn't come across?" Rapson inquired, somewhat casually. "What happens then—to me?"

"Well," Kebreau drawled, "we shall give you a good run for—our money! In the end, you'll be knocked on the head and perhaps end up in a cannibal stewpot. There are cannibals 'way back, you know! If you do, the feasters won't have the pleasure of all your body, because we shall have sent bits of it down to Monrovia in the event of too much hesitation there!"

"I see!" said Rapson, quietly. There was grim certainty in Kebreau's voice. "I see! A hand, a foot, or something of that sort, eh? Just to show you mean business!"

"Anybody would think," Kebreau sneered, "that you'd worked out the scheme with us! You've hit the thing right off, Rapson!"

"Well," said Rapson, with an assumption of cheerfulness he really did not feel, "while there's life there's hope! Being held to ransom means that a fellow is kept alive—for a time, anyway!"

"There isn't a hope for you!" put in Lingard. "Not a blasted hope, see, if those guys down at Monrovia don't come across with the dough!"

"Shut up, you!" snarled Kebreau and Lingard subsided.

Rapson laughed, shortly, mirthlessly.

"If they knew you needed it as badly as all this," he said, "they'd surely start a new bake-house— I mean mint—especially to make it for you. What about some grub? Not going to starve me, are you?"

CHAPTER XVI

HIGH POLITICS

"Although my company can afford to pay the twenty thousand pounds, sir, I consider that your Government should do so!" Mr. Darcy was pacing the floor of President Coolidge's room. He had brought in a ransom note which had been found on the dead body of Richardson by Dave Dawson, who had gone down post-haste when a telegraph message from Monrovia had asked why the train had not arrived.

President Coolidge sighed. Vice-President Lincoln pursed his full lips.

"We are sorry, Mr. Darcy!" It was Lincoln who spoke. "But as we keep telling you, the Government simply dare not let the ransom be paid. It would be regarded by the people as surrender to a man who is a public enemy!"

"But the people ought not to forget what Mr. Rapson's done for Liberia!" Darcy grated, angrily.

"A people's memory is proverbially short," said Mr. Lincoln, suavely. "The cry, if we paid the money, or allowed you to pay it, would be that we were providing Kebreau with the means to start another rebellion."

"Confound the cry, whatever it might be!" Darcy

exclaimed. "I shall appeal to the British Government!"

"What then?" Lincoln demanded. "Your Government, in the present state of international affairs, wouldn't take the risk of interfering in the internal affairs of Liberia. You have only to ask your Consul to find that out!"

"I'll go and see him!" Darcy decided, and hurried away. The British Consul heard his story, looked gravely at him. Then:

"I'm very sorry, Mr. Darcy," he said. "I'm afraid nothing can be done. The Liberian Government is within its rights. We can't do anything. As you're aware, there is no real diplomatic relationship between the two Governments—and the most surprising thing to the British Government is that you ever got the concession. I suspect that Mr. Coolidge, who has a regard for Britain, influenced the decision. But that's all he can do—he dare not allow money to be paid to Kebreau, and we can't force him to."

"So Rapson's to be left to the mercy of Kebreau?" Darcy rasped.

"I rather fancy," the Consul told him, "that if your company paid the money there'd be a great deal of complication and trouble. We are simply powerless! After all, you know, it's not a case of the Liberian Government acting against a British subject. If that were the case, then I've no doubt something could and would be done about it."

"To the devil with your politics!" Darcy snarled and went out of the room. He hurried to his own offices, where Dawson was waiting for him.

"Listen, Dave!" he said, and told him what had happened.

"God!" came from Dawson. "The ungrateful hounds! The company must do something, sir!"

"I know—and I'm going to do it for them!" snapped Darcy. "We've got five thousand pounds in cash. We've got the new 'plane on the landing-ground." It had been man-hauled from the harbour, ready for Rapson to pick up. "Kebreau wants the machine. Will you take it out—with a letter offering him five thousand pounds delivered immediately he agrees?"

"You get the letter written, sir!" Dawson answered. "I'll go and give the machine the look-over. Leave Rapson up there? My God, no!"

He was busy fuelling up when Darcy arrived.

"There'll be the devil to pay, Dawson," Darcy said. "But hang everybody!"

"There'd be a bigger devil to pay if Kebreau isn't paid—if he doesn't accept your offer, too, sir," Dawson grated. "Don't forget that he's threatened to tear up the line and keep on tearing it up."

"I told the President that," Darcy said. "But he's afraid! Afraid there'd be an uproar—perhaps a revolt led by someone other than Kebreau if he paid or agreed to our paying. But we'll do it, without permission. How soon can you be ready?"

"Another hour, sir!" Dawson told him. "I'll be able to get up country before six o'clock and leave the machine where indicated. It'll mean I shall have to camp out on my own for the night—shan't be able to start back, not even for the railway, until morning comes!"

An hour and a half later, Dawson took off from the landing-ground. A couple of lorries dashed towards the ground as the machine took off, and Frontier Force guards flung themselves out and raced towards Darcy, who was there to see Dawson off.

"Must have heard about my fiddling with the machine!" Dawson smiled, grimly. "Well, they're too darn late! I'm up, and I'm on my way!"

Flying solo, Dawson was feeling anything but hopeful. Kebreau's instructions were that any communication was to be flown up-country and left, with the aeroplane, in a clearing twenty or so miles from the railroad. Nothing was said about how an answer would be given.

"Because," grated Dawson, "he's probably certain the money will be paid. Then he'd simply turn Ted loose and let him find his way in, or, perhaps, have him escorted to the railway."

Kebreau had been very thorough in his directions: for with them was a section of a map, showing the spot at which the landing was to be made. He was safe in doing so, because it would take troops a long time to cut a way through the dense jungle, and, as Dawson realized, Kebreau was not likely to be anywhere near the spot, or at least, would be in a position whence he could see the approach of a number of men. He probably had natives out, natives who knew the narrow trails and who would bring him warning. It would be only after the pilot had left the machine that anybody would approach it—and that was not likely to be Kebreau himself!

Dawson followed his mapped course and at last saw the clearing, one of the many natural clearings to be found. He circled above it for a while, but could see no signs of life down below.

"Here goes!" he muttered at last. "I've got to chance everything—perhaps my life!"

He set the Moth down safely, but remained in the cockpit for a while. No one came from the surrounding jungle, however, and eventually Dawson got down. It was then that he expected somebody to put in an appearance, but nobody did.

"They won't while I'm around," he grated, and moved across the clearing. He had the sun to help him for a while, but when he entered the jungle, had to rely upon his compass for direction.

Shortly afterwards, as he slashed his way through the undergrowth, looking for a trail, he heard the thrum of a machine.

"God—they've come for it!" he exclaimed, and resisted the temptation to go back. He would be unable to do anything if he did return. A matter which puzzled him was why Kebreau had not left someone at the clearing to collect any letter or, as he may have hoped, money in the machine? Had the fellow expected the full twenty-thousand pounds to be handed over without any attempt at bargaining? It certainly looked like that. And where was the machine being taken?

"The swine's got another landing-place," snarled Dawson. "I might have expected that. Well, I can't

do anything except get as far away as I can and——"
He had stepped on to a forest trail a little while before.
Now, he came to a sudden halt. Half a dozen natives
were in front of him, every one of them armed. A
movement at the rear, and a glance over his shoulder
showed him several more men.

All except one of the men were scantily-clad natives:
the exception was a Negro, wearing uniform. He
spoke—in English.

"Give me any weapons you have," he said. "No
harm is intended you, because you are going as a
messenger."

Dave Dawson's hand came away from the revolver
it had gripped.

"So that's the way of it!" he snapped. "I was
allowed to get away so that the 'plane could be taken
off. Where's the message?"

"Your gun!" the Negro said, and Dawson handed
it over. There was a rush behind him, and the natives
searched him. All they found was a bush-knife.

"The message will be brought," he was told. "We
shall camp here and wait for it."

These natives evidently knew the jungle, for they
led the way to a small clearing. There, Dawson,
although not bound, knew that escape would be
impossible.

"How long have I got to wait?" he demanded, as
he sat beside a small fire.

"Until the morning," the uniformed Negro told
him. "General Kebreau has taken the machine
to——" He did not finish, but left his meaning clear,
nevertheless.

"So it was Kebreau who took it, eh?" growled Dawson. "Why—why didn't he send his message to me at once?"

"There was a reason," the answer came. "You will know it in good time."

The words held a sinister note, and Dawson had an icy feeling in the pit of his stomach.

CHAPTER XVII

GRIM TOKEN OF HATE

TED RAPSON, sitting against the bole of a tree, unbound because escape was impossible, with so many men about, jerked up at sound of an aeroplane. An hour or so before, Kebreau had left the little camp, following the arrival of a native who looked as if he had been running hard. Kebreau went without saying a word to Rapson, but Lingard and Woolf remained at camp.

At sound of the engine, Rapson became a prey to mingled thoughts. Kebreau had spoken about the Moth being part of the ransom: had it happened that the machine was being brought in accordingly? Or was the Moth simply out on a reconnaissance flight, looking for him? The latter idea died almost at birth, for Rapson knew the almost impossibility of the machine being able to locate this camp, hidden as it was in the jungle.

The drone of the engine died, and some time afterwards, Kebreau entered the clearing. There was a vicious look in his eyes as he strode to where Rapson was sitting, and Ted knew that whatever else the coming of the machine meant, it did not mean that the ransom money had been delivered.

"They must take me for a weak fool!" Kebreau snarled. He pulled out a pocket-book and tore a sheet of paper from it. He flung the paper down at Rapson's feet and began to unscrew the cap of his fountain-pen. "Write," he snapped, "and tell them I'm not bluffing! I asked for twenty thousand pounds—and they've offered me five!"

"I told you," Rapson said, with a wry smile, "nobody would believe me worth twenty thousand jimmy o' goblins! Take the five and don't be greedy—you've got the Moth, haven't you?"

"Yes, I've got the Moth!" said Kebreau. "And a promise of five thousand pounds—if I'll leave you on the railway."

"And you think they wouldn't put the money there for you, I suppose?" Rapson grinned.

"Damn them, they'd do that!" Kebreau assured him. "They'd do it because they know I'd tear the damn railway up if they didn't. But five thousand pounds! Bah! Write what I'm going to dictate!"

He handed the fountain-pen to Rapson, who took it.

"I can't help myself, can I?" Ted suggested. "Right —go ahead!"

It was a very brief note, which, at Kebreau's order, Ted signed with his own name. Then:

"Add a postscript!" Kebreau snapped. "Say: 'With this is my left hand—the right is to follow if the terms are not agreed to.'"

Rapson looked Kebreau full in the face. He shuddered when he saw the man's eyes.

"I won't be much use to them with only one hand, will I?" he managed to ask, quietly.

"But they'll pay!" Kebreau sneered. "The Government'll pay because the British Government will hold 'em responsible for your life! Write that postscript!"

Rapson did not use the pen for the purpose indicated. He sent it flying like a dart in a tavern taproom. It struck Kebreau in the top lip, and as he staggered away, Rapson sprang to his feet. He flung himself at Kebreau, kicked Lingard out of the way as the latter tried to stop him, and got his hand about the revolver in Kebreau's holster. But Woolf was there —and he twisted a leg between Rapson's. Ted went down, dragging Kebreau with him. On top, Kebreau's hands went around Ted's throat, but Alf Lingard, scrambling up on to hands and knees, smacked a revolver butt down on Ted's head and as he dropped into an abyss of unconsciousness, Rapson's last thought was: "Shall I wake up minus a hand?"

He awoke with two hands, but they were bound. Kebreau thrust the fountain-pen between his fingers.

"Write!" he said, harshly. Laboriously, Rapson wrote. "Just add to the postscript," Kebreau ordered. "It'll save time—keep them from fooling about. Say: 'I shall not be able to write another note, because a man can't very well write without a hand. Neither can he see without eyes.' That," Kebreau jeered at Rapson, "is to let 'em know that they're to expect your right hand if they don't come across. Your right hand—and your eyes."

Rapson felt very sick. He fought for equanimity. He somehow managed to put down the dreadful words, then the pen dropped from his fingers as Kebreau stooped and whipped up the paper. Ted jerked his bound hands close to his body.

"For God's sake don't do that, Kebreau!" he pleaded, and the rebel laughed.

"They'll pay—every cent of it!" he snarled, and a little later hurried from the camp. Night had not yet fallen, and Rapson, his head aching terribly, heard the drone of the aero-engine; it died away gradually, and he knew that Kebreau was on the way to deliver the threatening ultimatum. Ted knew that Dawson must have brought out the 'plane. He wondered where he was just now: perhaps waiting for Kebreau's message. Naturally, Kebreau would not allow Dawson to come to the camp and then go back. . . .

Kebreau grounded the Moth in the clearing where Dawson had left it. Dave Dawson, a good distance in the jungle, had heard the machine, and for a moment wondered whether it was bringing in Ted Rapson. Then he remembered the Negro's words: they meant that Dawson was to take out a message, not Rapson himself!

One of the natives slipped out of the clearing, and was absent for a good while. Before he returned, Dawson heard again the sound of the engine—heard it until it faded away in the distance.

Then the native came back. He carried a small parcel. It was addressed to Mr. Darcy.

"I'll keep it until the morning," said the uniformed Negro. "You'll have to be bound for the night," he told Dawson. "We're going to guide you through the jungle to a river. There's a canoe which will take you up to the railway. When you get there, it will be up to you to make your way to Monrovia."

"What's in that parcel?" Dawson demanded, anxiously.

"I don't know!" was the answer. "Better get to sleep—you've got a long journey ahead of you to-morrow!"

Dave Dawson slept only fitfully, and when, after a meagre meal at dawn, he set off with the natives, he was a bundle of nerves. He had the parcel in one of his pockets, and for some reason he was afraid of it. . . .

They reached a river. A canoe was drawn out from overhanging trees, and Dawson was made to get into it. Three natives went with him, two to paddle, the third to see that Dawson did not try any tricks. Occasionally, Dawson was made to take one of the paddles to relieve the men. Mile after mile the canoe slipped through the water. Now and then a native village was passed, but the canoe did not stop at any of them. When it did stop, it was away from any village. Then on again; and then, towards evening, Dawson was made to get out on to the bank.

"The river leads to the railway," he was told. "One of your bridges crosses it." The man backed away from the bank, turned the canoe and paddled back the way it had come.

"God!" breathed Dawson, and thrust his hand into his pocket. It touched the parcel there and he withdrew it, as though it had burnt his fingers. He did not know how far he was from the railway: the scenery was typical of most of the country, the river might be any one of those over which he had helped to throw bridges. He set off along the bank. Darkness fell and just before it did he saw the bridge.

"Those swines knew I'd get this far before it was too dark to see!" he snarled. "Well, this is something! I won't have to sleep in the jungle, but can camp down on the bridge until morning!"

But he did not camp down all night. He was not unduly tired, despite his restless night. He had rested fairly well while in the canoe. He managed to snatch a little sleep, lying on the bridge beside the track. Then, when he awakened, he set off down the line. He knew where he was now, and that a few miles along, there was a village, destined perhaps one day to be a town. There was a telegraph post in the village, as in several others along the railway. These posts were worked by Liberians and their main purpose was to make possible early discovery of the breaks in the wire caused by the natives.

Dawson staggered into the village, which might have been a place of the dead. It was past midnight. He went to the telegraph post and hammered on the door. The Liberian in charge should be inside.

"Hello,—who's there?" a voice called out, and a window opened.

"Dawson — Dawson of the Company!" Dave answered. "Oh, it's you, Mellor. Let me in, quickly, for God's sake!"

He almost stumbled into the room and flopped into a chair.

"Get through to Monrovia!" he ordered Mellor. "Directly to head office. Mr. Darcy was going to keep a man on all the time I've been away. Say that I want an engine to be sent up for me—then I'll tell you what else to say!"

Mellor began working his instrument. He connected head office.

"Mr. Darcy's at the other end, sir," he told Dawson.

"Ask him to have an engine got ready to leave," Dawson said. "Say I've got a message for him. Ask if I shall open it, and wire what it says. I'll be able to use the instrument myself in a few minutes."

His head was clearing somewhat now. He took grip on himself as he heard the chatter of the telegraph instrument.

"Mr. Darcy says you're to open the letter," Mellor spoke without looking up. "He's given orders for the engine to have steam got up."

"Good!" said Dawson and took the parcel out of his pocket. It was tied round with well-knotted string, which he cut with a knife borrowed from Mellor. When he pulled away the paper wrapping, he saw a roughly made box. He dragged the thin wood apart—and gasped at what was revealed. A folded sheet of bloodstained paper on top of a severed left hand.

"Oh, my God!" Dawson almost dropped the gruesome thing. His own hands trembled as he placed it on the desk, and took up the paper. With difficulty, because of the blood, he managed to read what was written on it and knew that Ted Rapson had written those words. Mellor gasped as his eyes fell on the severed hand.

"The swine! The inhuman devil!" Dawson shouted. "Listen, Mellor! You'll have to send the message— I can't!"

"Not with trembling hands, sir," Mellor said, shortly. "I'm ready, sir!"

Mr. Darcy sat beside his operator, Lanes, down in Monrovia. The operator wrote quickly as the instrument gave him the words that were being sent in. Darcy was reading them as they went down on paper.

"Kebreau refuses to compromise. The full twenty thousand pounds must be paid, otherwise I shall not be liberated and the line will be wrecked. The money in bullion is to be left at Sanoyeh Plain precisely at four o'clock on Thursday afternoon. Only an engine is to bring it up, and Kebreau will be up in the aeroplane to observe. I shall be delivered by parachute. Two hundred gallons petrol to be left as well. E. Rapson.

P.S. With this is a left hand—the right is to follow if the terms are not agreed to. I shall not be able to write another note, because a man can't very well write without a hand. Neither can he see without eyes. E.R."

Word by word Darcy read the message, and his tanned face went almost ashen.

"My God!" he exclaimed. "What——"

"Just a minute, sir!" came from Lanes. The instrument was still working, and once more Darcy's eyes picked out the words as Lanes jotted them down.

"Tell Darcy that there was a left hand with the note. Must be Rapson's, I feel sure, because his ring is on a finger. I think it will cost us more than twenty thousand pounds if Kebreau tears up the line. Gathered from a Negro that Kebreau's intention is to fly out of the country when he gets the gold. Suggest that Sierre Leone be communicated with and machines be on the look-out for the Moth. Looks as though Kebreau has given up idea of

rebellion. This should be conveyed to the Government—
may result in change of mind regarding payment of
ransom. Dawson."

Mr. Darcy snatched the flimsies from the desk.

"Keep in touch with Dawson!" he ordered Lanes.
"I'm going to see the President!"

The fact that it was not yet dawn did not effect
Darcy's decision: the matter was urgent enough,
serious enough, to justify arousing His Excellency.
Those few words of Dawson's regarding Kebreau's
plan, would at any rate be sufficient excuse. Darcy
hurried out of the building and through the dark,
grass-grown streets of Monrovia. The booming of the
surf drummed in his ears. Loose corrugated roofs
clanked. Discarded tins clattered along the streets.
Already men were at work stoking the engine, as
Darcy could hear. He came at last within sight
of the Executive Mansion and when he drew
nearer was challenged by the guard of the Frontier
Force.

"Mr. Darcy!" he answered. "I must see His
Excellency at once!"

"We cannot——" one of the guards began, but
Darcy rasped:

"You can, and must. Tell him that I have news of
Kebreau—important news!"

The assertion worked like magic. Anything to do
with Kebreau was warranted to do so. One of the
guards disappeared, was absent for a short time, and
when he returned, told Darcy to follow him. Darcy
did so and at last found himself inside the building.
He was escorted up the first flight of stairs and shown

N

into the President's office. His Excellency was in pyjamas: scarlet-and-yellow striped.

Darcy almost pressed the papers into the President's hand.

"From Kebreau!" he said, harshly. "I've got an engine being stoked."

Mr. Coolidge sat on the corner of his desk and read the messages. He read them with what was to Darcy irritating slowness. Presently he looked up:

"Where's the hand?" he asked.

"Where—— My God!" Darcy exploded, aghast at what he took to be callousness. "It——"

"Please be calm, sir," said Mr. Coolidge. "I really asked the question because, as surely you must realise, Kebreau could conceivably have tapped the wires and sent those messages!"

Mr. Darcy took a deep breath. "Those messages were sent by Dawson. He gave the code word before doing so. He has the—the hand. In view of what Dawson says he learnt, I insist on being allowed to send the ransom in full."

The President put the papers down beside him. "I agree, Mr. Darcy, that the situation is altered—if the information is correct. No one is more anxious than I am that Mr. Rapson should return safely."

"Minus a hand!" grated Darcy.

"But you will understand," His Excellency went on, "that I am not a dictator. I have to act constitutionally, and this is a matter for the consideration of the Government as a whole. I suggest that you send for Mr. Dawson. I wish to have the—the hand here to show to my colleagues, some of whom, as you know only too well, are absolutely opposed to giving over so much money to Kebreau. Possibly, when they hear Mr. Dawson's story, they may change their minds. In any case, there is plenty of time, isn't there? The bullion and petrol could be got to Sanoyeh by four o'clock on Thursday. I promise you my full support!"

"Thank you, sir!" Darcy said, and moved towards the door. The President stopped him.

"I shall call a meeting for first thing in the morning, Mr. Darcy. As soon as Mr. Dawson arrives, please bring him here."

Darcy promised to do so, and went away.

"I suppose," he murmured, as he hurried to the little station, "I suppose he's right. Kebreau could have tapped the wire, but I know he didn't. However, Rapson's handwriting will settle any doubts some of the damned Government may voice! Poor Rapson—victim of political junketing!"

CHAPTER XVIII

1437—AGAIN

TED RAPSON, lying in the tent in the kidnapper's camp, tossed about in the throes of a touch of fever. Those two knocks on the head had not done him much good. He was raving about his hand: in his nightmare, he remembered what Kebreau had said, and made him write, about his left hand. Now he was in delirium—and fighting, it seemed to him, with a bloodied stump of an arm which left nasty smears on the grinning faces which he struck. He had spaces of more or less consciousness, and at such times Kebreau or one of the others would dose him with quinine, so that the very worst of the fever passed, but left him a trembling wreck.

He felt at his left wrist and smiled grimly. He wished he had a gun, or even a knife.

The hours passed, the night gave place to day, and he was allowed to move about the camp, keen eyes watching him all the time. Night settled down again and Rapson was driven into the tent set apart for him. Natives squatted on guard outside, the tent flap open so that they could see inside. Beyond them, Rapson could see the larger tent that was occupied by Kebreau and Lingard and Woolf. Watching them, with some bottles on an upturned box for table, Rapson remembered that scene on which he had looked just before he brought disaster on Washington. There had been a difference, however: then, he had been a free man. Now he was bound, a prisoner without a hope of escape.

"None!" Rapson gritted. 'Yet, somewhere at hand, is the Moth! But what good would it be if I reached it? Before I could get it warmed up, no doubt these fellows would be on me!"

Besides which, he did not know where the machine was. He had a fair idea of the direction, because of the sound it had made when coming in and the point at which Kebreau had entered camp. Yet the landing-place might be a mile or so away—and to find the trail to it would be impossible, at least during the night hours.

On the other hand, Rapson knew that his sole hope lay in escaping. He did not trust Kebreau. That statement in the letter he had dictated, about delivering his prisoner by parachute, did not deceive Rapson, who had long since sized up the man who had essayed to be President of the Black Republic. Treacherous— the word summed up his character. The depositing of the ransom would mean, Rapson felt convinced, that he would be pitched out of the Moth with a parachute fixed so that he could not open it. Kebreau was on safe ground: he knew it was impossible for the Frontier Force to trace him to his lair without warning being given in time by the numerous native scouts scattered through the jungle. At the first alarm, Kebreau would be off in the Moth—after killing his prisoner! And if duplicity was tried by those of whom ransom was demanded, and they left junk instead of bullion, well,

Kebreau would have had his revenge in advance by sending Rapson to certain death. . . .

He fought against the bonds that held him, but might as well have spared himself for all the effect he made. The chattering of the natives gradually ceased as many of them fell asleep. The fire outside Kebreau's tent showed him and his two companions still at their drinking. The night sounds of the jungle began. Depression settled on Rapson—to be relieved, an hour or so after Kebreau's tent-flap had been dropped, by the pressure of a hand on his shoulder as he lay against the side of the tent. For a moment, Rapson thought that he was dreaming. Then the pressure increased, as if someone was trying to rouse him. Rapson moved his shoulder slightly—hope in his heart, although he could not understand who could be there to succour him.

"No noise, sah!" It was a native's voice which spoke beneath the canvas. "I help you get away!"

Rapson's answer was another movement of his shoulder. He went hot and cold by turns and thought he was beginning another malaria bout. Then the unseen hand moved down his arm and Rapson understood the action. He lifted his bound arms and then felt something at the bonds. A knife. . . . The bonds dropped from his arms, and his hands were free. Free, but aching. The knife was put into one of them, and he hunched up and leant over, sliced through the ropes about his ankles.

"This way, sah! Under tent!" The voice spoke again. Rapson turned and realized that the canvas was being forced up: obviously the native had eased one of the guy-ropes.

Perspiring now, Rapson went flat on his stomach and began to worm his way beneath the canvas, inch by inch, waiting now and then, heart in mouth, to listen. Then farther out—and at last he was standing up outside.

"Who are you?" he breathed at the vague shadow before him.

"A friend, sah!" was the only answer. "You come!"

It was no time for fuller information to be asked or given. Rapson allowed himself to be led away from the tent. Not walking, but crawling, almost wriggling, across the clearing around which he knew numerous natives were lying asleep.

Then he and his rescuer were amongst the trees, and on their feet.

"Come!" the native said again, and held Rapson's arm and piloted him through the darkness. They did not walk quickly, but slowly and cautiously, aware that a wakeful native might hear any sound they should make. They stepped on to a beaten track, and the going was easier thenceforth; and they made better progress.

All this time, Rapson had not spoken, nor been spoken to. Now, however, he asked:

"Who are you and why have you helped me?"

"I am Duli," was the answer, but it meant nothing to Rapson. "Duli—No. 1437."

It registered! 1437! The native workman who had hidden Blakey's letter in the hole on the river bank! Rapson stopped walking.

"I don't understand!" he said, hoarsely, but Duli implored him not to stand still.

"I will tell, sah!" he said. "Come."

"Is this a—a trap of some kind?" Rapson did not feel sure of the native. "Where are you taking me?"

"To your machine, sah!" Duli answered, and Rapson almost gasped.

"Go ahead, then!" he managed to say, and followed Duli down the dark aisle of the forest.

At last Duli came to a halt. He forced an opening in the scrub, and went out, followed by Rapson. The latter saw that they were in a wide clearing. A crescent moon rode overhead.

"The machine, sah!" said Duli, and pointed to a dark blotch in the clearing. Rapson almost ran over to it, and when he reached the spot, knew that Duli had not been lying. No. 1437 was at his heels.

"Take me with you, sah?" he asked, eagerly. "Kebreau he kill me."

"Just a minute," said Rapson. "Why did you help me get away?"

"Kebreau kick my backside, sah," was the reply. "Because I ask for bottle of gin." And Ted Rapson laughed, not incredulously, but understandingly. A white man might, perhaps, kick a native without arousing anger, but a Negro—no! And, as Rapson saw things, Duli no doubt considered that he had a right to be treated decently by Kebreau. Had he not lost a job on the railway by helping Kebreau? A bottle of gin was, surely, small enough price to pay for that! True, there may have been other bottles, and Duli's requirements in the way of poison—traders' gin is somewhat different from that served at London's cocktail parties!—may have proved rather heavy.

"What do you think would happen to you in Monrovia, if I took you, Duli?" Rapson asked, grimly.

"I save your life, sah!" Duli said, simply.

"Don't you know," Rapson asked, "that by leaving that letter for Kebreau you caused the death of a lot of men? Besides which, in a way, we're already quits. I saved you from the leopard, didn't I?"

"That the reason I help, sah!" said Duli, simply.

While he was speaking, Rapson had clambered up into the cockpit. But he got out again and stood in front of Duli. He knew that he was being ungrateful —but, after all, it might be better for Duli to try to get away, not go down to Monrovia. The Government would, probably, be little inclined to deal leniently with him. Other natives who had taken sides with Kebreau, and who had been arrested, had found little mercy. . . .

"Listen to me, Duli!" Ted Rapson said. "I don't feel so sure about people being kind to you in Monrovia. In a way, I don't mean a great deal to the Government."

"I take chance, sah!" was Duli's rejoinder. "Plenty people in with Kebreau and they kill me if they find out I help you."

"Go back, and he won't suspect you," Rapson suggested.

"Maybe too late do that, sah." Duli was no innocent, apparently.

"But Kebreau told me he's going to leave the country!" Rapson tried again.

"He not leave country, sah!" Duli said. "He only tell that. I hear him say money not paid if people

think he stay in country. He going drop bombs on
Monrovia, sah. Plenty bombs he got. If he paid
he let you fall dead from machine, then go and bomb
town."

Rapson scratched his head. Was Duli merely saying
this in order to force agreement to take him out?
Or was he telling the truth? Kebreau had sounded
convincing when he had said he meant to get out
of the country, but, on the other hand, he might
intend to have a last fling, bomb Monrovia and then
take wing to some safe destination!

"Do you know where he's got the bombs, Duli?"
Rapson asked, suddenly.

"No, sah!" was the answer.

"If I take you out, would you lead men to where
Kebreau is now?" Rapson tried another course.

Duli laughed, or, rather, giggled. Liberians are
given to giggling. Often enough they end an argument with a giggle, and leave the other fellow wondering who had had the better of it.

"Kebreau not stay there when find you gone, sah,"
he said. "Then he smash railway, sah."

"God, yes! I forgot that!" Rapson exclaimed.
Kebreau could carry on a very troublesome guerilla
warfare which would cost the company thousands,
tens of thousands, of pounds; perhaps, indeed, hold
up the work for months, and, maybe, longer. Even
the possession of the aeroplane now did not mean
that Rapson was in a position to take effective action
against Kebreau, near though his camp was. Hidden
in the jungle, it could not be located—and besides,
Rapson had no weapons of any kind, except the knife

which Duli had given him and he still retained. By the time he had flown down to Monrovia, Kebreau would be gone. The Frontier Force could search the jungle for weeks without hoping to get on his trail.

Suddenly, Rapson clicked thumb and finger together, so sharply that Duli jumped.

"Listen to me," Rapson jerked. "I've got an idea, Duli! If you're willing to help, and—and things turn out all right, I'll take you down to Monrovia and do the best I can for you."

"I listen, sah," Duli said. "Why you not start machine?"

"Not yet!" Rapson said, grimly. "Here's the idea, Duli!" and he spent the next few minutes in a quiet explanation. Duli listened intently, and now and again Rapson heard him whistle softly.

"Are you willing?" Rapson ended. "I know there's a risk, but if you can't get into camp or can't get back, do the best you can to hide. Later on, come up to me on the railway and I'll fix something for you. If you can get into camp before my escape is discovered, everything should turn out all right, I think."

"I try, sah," Duli promised.

"Right—I'll give you half an hour, then I'll start up the engine," said Rapson, and Duli scurried away.

He slipped into the scrub, on to the track, down which he hurried, soft-footed, with ears attuned to every sound. Rapson had given him half an hour, in which time Duli should be able to make camp. Duli knew he could make it sooner than that, since he had not the encumbrance of the white man. He realized, as Rapson had realized, that the escape might be discovered, and then men would be coming down the trail. Kebreau's first thought would be for the Moth. Even although Rapson did not know where the machine was, Kebreau would not be inclined to leave it unguarded now.

But Duli reached camp well within the half-hour allotted to him. He slid out of the scrub and laid down where he could watch the two guards outside the tent from which Rapson had crawled. The flap was still open, but Rapson had told Duli that he had left the blanket crumpled up, with his topee at one end: a shape calculated to deceive the guards unless they went into the tent. The fact that the camp was still asleep told Duli that no visit had been paid to the tent during the last hour. He knew that one of the guards had gone in a little before he had awakened Rapson; Duli had chosen his time accordingly, because visits were not very frequent or close together.

Suddenly the two guards leapt to their feet; and Duli knew why. They yelled—other men sprang up. Kebreau came running out of his tent, Linguard and Woolf at his heels.

For the silence of the jungle had been broken by the muffled drone of an engine.

In that quiet solitude, the sound of the Moth's engine travelled far.

One of the guards had dashed into Rapson's tent —he came out, a blanket dangling in his hand. He kicked the topee along the ground and it rolled to Kebreau's feet.

"Gone, sah, gone!" the guard shrilled, and Kebreau clouted him on the side of the head with the barrel of a revolver.

"All men parade!" Kebreau yelled, and someone flung dry tinder on the nearly dead fire. The natives sprang to attention, and Kebreau tabbed them off. All were present, and the job did not take many minutes.

"Follow me!" Kebreau roared and burst from the camp. He was half drunk, as were Lingard and Woolf, but the alarm had served to pull them together somewhat. Behind them, the natives ran down the trail, the sound of the engine louder the farther they ran.

"He can't take off for some time!" Kebreau yelled, "The engine's got to warm up! God! It's stopped!"

Five minutes later, the engine sounded again—Ted Rapson was carrying out the plan he had made. Every now and then he cut off the engine, to make Kebreau, if Kebreau was coming, think that something was wrong with it. The engine did not need half an hour to warm up sufficiently to take off,—and Rapson did not want to take off, yet! He had given Duli half an hour, however, because there was the chance that the escape had been discovered and that Kebreau's men were on the way.

Again and again the engine stopped, then roared up again. Kebreau snarled viciously:

"He's not going to get away, the swine! When we get there, everybody's to make an attack on the rear of the 'plane! Understand? The rear? You don't want to get cut to pieces by the propeller!"

"And the 'plane wouldn't be much use without it!'" came from Lingard, who knew that Kebreau's concern was not for his men but the machine.

"Shut up!' growled Kebreau, and prodded him with his rifle. "Some of you will hang on to the tail, and the rest of us will climb up and get at Rapson! He hasn't got a gun! That engine's stopped again!"

The almost deafening roar had ceased. The little band of men was very near to the clearing by now. Duli, trotting along with the rest, his rifle on his shoulder, was not feeling altogether happy. He knew that the critical moment was yet to come. He had succeeded in getting into camp and no one had suspected him. But could Rapson carry out his plan? Duli, although he had agreed to play his part, felt that Rapson was by way of being a fool not to have gone away while he could. Staying behind was to take a risk, a great risk. A little giggle came from Duli's throat. It was his substitute for a shrug of the shoulders. After all, this Englishman might be a fool, but he was a brave one.

A low command came from Kebreau and the little band halted.

"Some of you move to the right," Kebreau ordered. "You'll jump out at different points and then rush the machine. The tail, remember! And go quietly, so that Rapson doesn't hear you—until you're at the machine. Come on!"

CHAPTER XIX

THE SURGE OF THE PRIMITIVE

NOT a sound was made by the little company as they completed the journey down trail to the edge of the clearing. They went on to their stomachs then and crawled towards the machine, whose engine was roaring, and had been, for the past five minutes without interruption.

Duli had manoeuvred so that he was at the end of the file, the first man in which presently reached the machine. Others moved up to him. Duli saw Kebreau, Lingard and Woolf get up and leave the crowd and move along the side of the 'plane. He raised his rifle and fired. One of the men—in the darkness Duli did not know whether it was Kebreau or one of his companions—crashed to earth—and instantly, all was confusion. Also, a rifle spurted orange flame beneath the machine, near one of the landing wheels, and a second man went down.

A native in front of Duli spun round and would have shot him, had not Duli got in first. Then Duli was in amongst the crowd, yelling that he had killed the man who gave the alarm. It was doubtful whether, with the sound of the engine loud above everything, anyone understood what Duli said, and there was no time to argue. More shots were coming from beneath the 'plane and Duli saw a man clambering up the machine. He could not make out who the man was, except that it was not Rapson, who had no hat. Natives crashed before the fire from the unseen marksmen, others tried to get him, Duli sprang up after the man on the machine—saw, with a sense of foreboding, that it was Kebreau. The latter had opened the cockpit door—and Duli pressed his rifle against the rebel's right shoulder and fired. Kebreau went head first into the cockpit.

Duli slipped in after him and as Kebreau squirmed to get up, struck him on the back of his head with the butt-ended rifle. Kebreau lay still. Duli turned in time to thrust his rifle-butt into the face of a man who had climbed up and was about to fire at him with a revolver. Alf Lingard lost his balance and thudded to the ground. His right arm had been shattered by a bullet, and his reaction, of dropping gun from left hand and making a grab for a hold, had not been quick enough.

Duli saw his erstwhile companions surrounding the machine, their rifles flashing. He saw that, instead of trying to rush Ted Rapson, who, as Duli knew, was under the machine, they had scattered to a distance: after all, they had no leaders now. Kebreau was unconscious, in the cockpit. Lingard was doing a sprint across the clearing—Duli did not know that Lingard had lost his revolver in his fall and had not stayed to look for it. Woolf was lying still, very still, where he had fallen at Rapson's first shot.

And from beneath the Moth Rapson was still using the rifle which Duli had left him, and to replace which Duli had resorted to swift action during the commotion consequent on the outbreak of alarm at the camp. Duli pumped a few shots at the blazing rifles and Rapson realized that it was time for him to do something. Only Duli could be firing at the enemy. Rapson let Lingard have a bullet which dropped him: Ted did not know it was Lingard, but a uniformed man meant an enemy more dangerous than the natives.

"That other fellow's Woolf—I saw his white face," Rapson grated. "But where's Kebreau?" He had not seen Kebreau climb on to the machine, for the rebel leader had straddled the end of the 'plane and edged his way up to the cockpit, followed by Duli.

Now, Rapson, his last shot fired, moved snail-like from the cover of the landing wheel. Then he suddenly sprang to his feet, and although bullets whanged about him, fired, fortunately, by inexpert riflemen, he managed to clamber up the side of the machine, yelling to Duli above the roar of the engine, to let him know who was coming.

Duli almost dragged him inside and in doing so stumbled over the hunched figure of Kebreau behind him. Rapson switched on the lights of the instrument board and saw—Kebreau.

"God! You got him, Duli!" he yelled, and used the rebel as a stepping-stone to the pilot's seat. Rapson dropped into it—and then realized that he was faced with a great problem. Out there on the ground were sinister humps. From some of them spurting flames issued, from others—nothing. Right ahead they were, potential wreckers of a taxying 'plane, but Rapson knew there was nothing for it but to take the chance. The moon was still shining and gave a fair amount

o

of light, fortunately. Kebreau would have chosen this place because of its comparative smoothness; Rapson's chance of making a take-off was commensurate with his ability to hold the 'plane down to a zig-zag course to avoid the immovable heaps out there.

He drew Duli's head down as, for a second, he throttled the engine.

"Bind Kebreau with something—get in back with him!"

Then the engine roared again, and Rapson took off the brakes. The Moth leapt forward—with rifles pumping bullets at it as before. A man leapt to life —and sprinted away, missed by a few inches as the machine roared past him. Rapson ruddered vigorously and gave the engine a burst—and a black heap shot by. Straight ahead, a man who had a split second before fired at the machine, streaked for safety. Twice more Rapson had to zig-zag before the whole of his tense body received the information that the moment had come when the 'plane would take off.

He dared not try to change course then, not even although there was another of those unmoving heaps in front. He had the stick pushed fully forward, throttle right open, and tail rising into level position. The moment had come for the slight backward release of the stick. Rapson eased the stick, the 'plane took off—and for a moment he had a horrible feeling that disaster was on him after all. But, instead, the machine roared over the inert body that lay on the ground—and Rapson could have yelled with triumph.

He scarcely realized it, but natives were still firing at the machine. It was a scream, shrill above the

A MAN LEAPT TO LIFE—AND SPRINTED AWAY

Facing page 210.

roar of the engine, which brought the fact home to him. He threw a glance over his shoulder, saw, in the light from the dashboard, Duli lying on top of Kebreau.

As Rapson looked, Duli moved, seemed to be trying to force himself up. Rapson turned away. He was not yet out of danger. Far ahead was a hill—and he dared not turn off so soon after leaving the ground. He held the stick back and got the 'plane into a good climb, and presently flattened out and went into a bank.

The rest was easy. By compass reading he obtained his course and flew in the direction in which he knew the railway lay. He climbed no higher than was necessary to over-top the jungle giants, and at last he made out the wide clearance through which the line ran.

He had looked round several times. Duli was lying on top of Kebreau still, and was making no effort to get up. Rapson was able to see that Kebreau's wrists were bound.

"Even if he's alive and comes round," Rapson gritted, "he'll not be any trouble! My God, but this is a finale Kebreau had never expected! Nor I, for that matter! The swine never intended handing me over alive!" Rapson shuddered at the thought of the narrow escape he had had. There was a wry, mirthless smile that was almost a grin on his face. "A kick instead of a bottle of gin saved me! Saved me and put done to Kebreau and all his damn business!"

The Moth had enough petrol to take him to the

coast, and as he drew near, he realized that all his troubles were not yet over. Nobody in Monrovia would expect him. The sound of the engine would suggest but one thing to them: that Kebreau was in the sky. The Frontier Force would be called out, and their rifles and machine-guns would be waiting for him. And even if they withheld their fire, Rapson would have nothing to help in landing. The field would be in darkness. Even the moon had gone in by now, and the African night was as black as the bottom of a deep, unfathomable pit.

"What the devil!" he grated. "I've got away and I must chance things now! God! There's the lighthouse!"

The intermittent flashes of Monrovia's solitary lighthouse, which warns ships of the treacherous rocks against which the surf beats and pounds, was a thing of beauty to Ted Rapson. It was a scintillating jewel in a black velvet setting. A tiny jewel as yet, which glowed, then disappeared, and glowed again. A beacon of welcome. . . .

Dave Dawson, asleep in Darcy's house, was awakened by the roar of an engine. He sat up in bed, then sprang to the window. Somebody rapped on his door, and then opened it. Darcy came in.

"Heavens above, what's this mean, Dawson?" Darcy jerked. "Would Kebreau——"

"That isn't Kebreau!" snapped Dawson, who was pulling on his breeches. "He wouldn't come. Why should he? The time limit expires to-day at four o'clock. He'd have nothing to gain by coming. God Almighty, sir, but I reckon Rapson must have managed to get away. Go and get dressed. I'm off to the landing-field!"

He slipped into his tunic and drew on his boots. He did not stay to put on puttees. If that was Rapson, he would be needing flares at the landing-field, and the sooner they were going the better.

Dawson ran into the street. Other people were there already, worried people who imagined that the 'plane meant trouble. Darcy's car stood beside the house, and Dawson sprang into it, started it, had the engine going when Darcy came from the house. He climbed in beside Dawson. People scattered before the car when it shot into the street. Potholes in the road meant nothing to Dawson. The car bumped into them, bumped out again, but Dawson was going full out—with the roar of the Moth high above. As he drove, Dawson switched off the headlights, switched them on again. It was a dexterous piece of work he was doing: signalling in morse. "D-a-w-s-o-n. D-a-w-s-o-n."

Half-clad people pursued the car, but it reached the landing-field well ahead of them. Meanwhile, Rapson, who had circled the town with engine full out, now climbed higher. He had seen and succeeded in reading Dawson's signals, and knew that he was safe. He climbed and flew around until he saw stationary lights at the landing-field. They streaked across the ground. Rapson throttled down and went into a glide which took him down to the field, into the stream of light from the car. The Moth taxied to a standstill and Rapson saw a crowd racing towards it. He opened the door, but before he was down, Dawson and Darcy were there.

"God—thank God!" Dawson cried, and almost kissed him. Darcy pump-handled Ted's arm until it ached. People cheered—and then the Terror burst.

Rapson knew, the moment he heard cheers change to curses. He jerked round, but was too late. A Negro had looked into the cockpit, and seen—Kebreau. With an animal-like cry he was in, others clambering up the machine to follow him at the news he had shouted down to them. Before getting out of the machine, Rapson had had a look at Duli: the unfortunate native was dead. Whether the shrieking Negroes knew this, Rapson was never certain. . . .

"Kebreau's in there!" he yelled at Dawson, and then was battering at black glistening faces and hard bullet heads, trying to get to the machine. But he and Dawson and Darcy were overwhelmed. Primitive passions were roused. Some of these people had lost friends, relatives, as the result of Kebreau's rising.

Shots rang out.

Rapson, struggling to free himself from half a dozen men, saw rifle flashes, heard the whistle of bullets overhead, and understood. The Frontier Force had arrived and was warning the crowd to clear off by firing over their heads. But these people were something less than human just now: they were sub-humans of the jungle. Even the Frontier Force squad was driven off and, perhaps because they were possessed by the same lust for immediate vengeance, they refrained from firing into the crowd.

Dawson fought free and reached Rapson, who was on the ground now, trying to struggle out of the grasp of several Negroes.

"Let up!" Dawson grabbed at two of the men and flung them aside. "Let——"

"Hooray! Hooray!" A mighty cheer, which had in it the blood-lust of hounds which had made the kill, broke out above everything else. Dawson turned —and felt sick. Held above the crowd was a dripping horror that a few moments before had been the head of a living man: Kebreau's head, hacked from his body by men in whom the animal had triumphed.

"God!" Rapson gasped, standing beside Dawson. That blood-lust cheering had made his assailants spring away from him. They were now, with scores of others, surging towards the man who was holding the gruesome token of vengeance.

"Let's get away! Mr. Darcy!" Dawson dragged Ted to where, ashen faced in the light of the car, Mr. Darcy was standing.

"The machine!" Rapson gasped. "They'll——"

"Damn the machine!" snarled Dawson. "They'll not do anything to it, I reckon. If they do, well, let 'em! We can't stay here—God knows what devilish things they'll be up to next!" He almost dragged Rapson to where the car was standing, almost flung him into it.

"Hey, you!" he barked at a couple of the Frontier Force. "Guard that 'plane!" and then the engine roared, he slipped in the gears and the car shot forward. Men sprang out of its path. Dawson swung round on two wheels and sent it tearing away from the field towards which more people were rushing.

"Thank God Duli was dead!" Dawson looked sharply at Rapson as the latter gasped out the words.

"What the devil d'you mean?" he cried, and Rapson told him.

"Those devils might have treated him the same as they did Kebreau!" Rapson rasped, as the car drew up outside the Executive Mansion, whither it had been decided to go. "I'm glad I made sure he was dead before I got him down, Dave!" He laughed, almost hysterically, as Frontier Force guards levelled rifles at them. The Mansion was surrounded by armed men. An officer shouted a demand to know who was in the car.

It was Rapson who answered him, and the officer almost ran up to the car.

"Take us to the President at once!" Ted rapped.

"His Excellency is inside with several members of the Government!" the officer said. "We thought Kebreau might be in the aeroplane and——"

"Thought! My God, thought!" mouthed Rapson. "He was—and now he's a dismembered horror!"

Some of the Frontier Force guards at that broke rank and went streaking away, like children who had heard the fanfare of a circus procession. The officer shouted after them, but they took no notice.

"Come on, gentlemen!" he said to the three whites, and led them to a door. He knocked, waited a moment or two, then the door was opened. Another officer stood there—he recognized Rapson and for a moment remained speechless. Then he stepped forward impulsively, hand outstretched.

He was one of the officers who had helped train the Railway Defence Force, and had become very friendly with Rapson.

"It seems impossible, sir!" he said. "But I'm pleased to see you."

"Take us to the President, please!" exclaimed Mr. Darcy.

"I—I'll go and announce you, sir," the officer answered. "Please come in!"

They entered. The door was closed. The officer raced up the stairs. He did not race down again, but a few moments later stood at the top and shouted at them to go up. They went up. President Coolidge, Mr. Lincoln, and a couple of other Ministers, were at the President's door.

His Excellency shook Rapson's hand, and a moment or so later all were in his room.

"I cannot say, Mr. Rapson," the President was smiling, as he spoke, "how pleased we are to see you. We—ah—we thought Kebreau had come in for some murderous reason!"

Ted Rapson pulled himself together.

"Kebreau did come, sir," he heard himself saying. "But not for a murderous reason. He didn't come willingly, either. He——"

President Coolidge, struck dumb by Rapson's statement, managed at last to find tongue.

"Kebreau—where is he?" he shouted, Presidential dignity dropping from him.

"He's dead—torn to pieces at the landing-field!"

rapped Ted. "He was alive when I brought him in. The people tore him limb from limb and——"

President Coolidge's dark eyes flashed.

"You let the mob get him?" he demanded.

"Let the mob!" Dave Dawson snapped out the words. "We didn't have a chance to stop them. They damn nearly treated us the same! Even the guards couldn't hold 'em back!"

Ted Rapson saw a bottle and a syphon on the table as the President moved. He stepped forward and seized the bottle.

"I'm sorry—help yourself, Mr. Rapson!" the President said, and Ted, with a short laugh, poured himself a stiff drink which he downed neat. The spirit burnt his throat, but steadied his nerves, killed the queer feeling he had had of wanting to scream with laughter.

"Your hand—your left hand!" President Coolidge stared at the hand which was holding the glass into which Rapson was pouring another drink.

Ted lifted the glass.

"Yes, Kebreau said he was going to cut it off, sir. I had a touch of fever and dreamed it was off. Why he didn't carry out his threat I don't know."

"But—but he sent your—he sent a left hand!" the President choked. "It—Mr. Dawson said your ring was on it."

"Yes, Kebreau pulled the ring off," Ted smiled, drily. "I suppose it was to make my friends believe the hand was mine. I guess it belonged to a German named Schwartz. Perhaps Kebreau had a warped sense of humour. Maybe he wanted to show you, when he dropped me in a parachute I wouldn't have been

able to open, that he'd bluffed you when he made
me write that my left hand was accompanying the
demand note. I don't know."

"Perhaps Mr. Rapson will tell us what happened?"
Lincoln made the suggestion and so lessened the
tension. Ted downed his second drink, and dropped
into a chair. He waited until the others were seated,
and then began to recount the story of events up
to the moment when he stepped out of the Moth at
the landing-ground.

"And that's all, gentlemen," he wound up. "Except
that if it's possible, I should like something to be
done for any dependants of Duli. It was he who saved
me, poor devil."

"I assure you, Mr. Rapson," said the President,
"that every effort shall be made to trace the poor
fellow's family. Liberia owes a lot to him."

"If it hadn't been that Duli was willing to help
me, Kebreau would still be alive," said Rapson.
"My plan was for him to get back to Kebreau's camp
if possible. He left me his rifle and some ammunition.
He succeeded in getting another weapon, as he hoped.
The idea was that I should start up the engine after a
time to arouse the camp. Duli would, of course, come
out with the rest, and he was to shoot to let me know
when they were approaching the 'plane. I was then
going to leave the machine and get to a place from
where I could pick off Kebreau. I hoped that would
throw the others into confusion, during which Duli
could reach the machine with me. As it wouldn't be
possible for me to pick out Kebreau in the darkness,
Duli was going to give the signal by firing his rifle

when he was right alongside Kebreau. But things didn't happen that way. Actually, I had got down from the cockpit, leaving the engine running, because I thought Kebreau must be near. I wanted to get into position. But Kebreau was nearer than I thought, for almost as I reached ground, I saw movements across the clearing. I had no time to do anything except drop behind one of the landing wheels. Then I just had to wait—until things happened."

"You didn't expect to get Kebreau, then?" Mr. Coolidge asked.

"Not alive," Rapson admitted. "I did hope, however, to finish him off. I didn't know how to engineer things so that I could take him prisoner. The position," he smiled ruefully, "was somewhat awkward! Kebreau just walked into trouble, as it happened, by getting on to the machine. Duli followed him and plugged him. I heard the thud, or, rather, I should say I felt the machine rock when someone dropped into the cockpit, and then, when a rifle fired from it, knew Duli at any rate was there. As I'd dropped—I believe I killed—Lingard, and Woolf was also down, I reckoned Kebreau must be in the machine. A native wouldn't have got into it, I imagined. So there we are—and Kebreau's finished!"

A babel of voices followed: men were congratulating Rapson on his escape and thanking him. Mr. President thumped his desk for silence.

"Not only is Kebreau finished," he said, "but I hope that Liberia's troubles are at an end. Mr. Rapson tells us that Kebreau had intended, on getting the ransom, to drop him to death, and then fly over and bomb Monrovia before clearing out of the country. Liberia will not forget, Mr. Rapson!" He stood up and took Ted's hand. "I hope," he said, "that from now on you will be able to proceed with your work without more worry than is normally contingent on it."

The words sounded somewhat banal to Rapson, who, however, merely said—and knew he was being just as trite:

"Thank you, sir. I hope so, too!"

He looked at Darcy.

"Yes," the latter understood. "I think we'll go now, and see if everything's all right with the 'plane!"

The three white men left the Mansion and piled into Darcy's car, but before they could start off, two Frontier Force men came up at the double.

"Ah, we were sent to tell you that the mob has gone away and the aeroplane is safe," one of them told Darcy. "But some of our men are still on guard there."

"Thanks," said Darcy, crisply. "Get going, Dawson! I'll bet Ted wants——"

"A wash and a good meal!" Rapson broke in.

And nobody told him, nobody had the heart to tell him, that the Government, which had just thanked him, would have allowed him to remain in Kebreau's hands. For, despite what the President had said about altered circumstances, Mr. Darcy had felt sure that the result of the Ministerial meeting would have been a refusal to meet Kebreau's demand for the ransom.

"Just as well," Darcy reflected. "Just as well to let Rapson remain ignorant of that. A man can smash two attempts at revolt—and the Government he's helped would desert him in his extremity! Bah!"

"What, sir?" Dawson glanced over his shoulder at the unconscious explosion.

"Nothing!" Darcy answered. "I was only—thinking!"

THE ACE SERIES

COMPLETE LIST OF TITLES

3s. 6d. *net per volume*

DESPOT OF THE WORLD	G. E. Rochester
JACKALS OF THE CLOUDS	G. E. Rochester
PIRATES OF THE AIR	G. E. Rochester
FLYING COWBOYS	G. E. Rochester
AIR RANGERS	G. E. Rochester
THE TRAIL OF DEATH	G. E. Rochester
THE BLACK SQUADRON	G. E. Rochester
THE FLYING SPY	G. E. Rochester
THE FLYING BEETLE	G. E. Rochester
CAPTAIN ROBINHOOD—SKYWAYMAN	G. E. Rochester
BLACK HAWK	G. E. Rochester
WINGS OF DOOM	G. E. Rochester
GREY SHADOW	G. E. Rochester
THE BULLDOG BREED	G. E. Rochester
BROOD OF THE VULTURE	G. E. Rochester
SKY PIRATES OF LOST ISLAND	G. E. Rochester
DERELICT OF THE AIR	G. E. Rochester
SCOTTY OF THE SECRET SQUADRON	G. E. Rochester
VULTURES OF DEATH	G. E. Rochester
SECRET SQUADRON IN GERMANY	G. E. Rochester
SQUADRON WITHOUT A NUMBER	G. E. Rochester
NORTH SEA PATROL	G. E. Rochester
LYNX V.C.	"Vigilant"
LYNX—SPYFLYER	"Vigilant"
LYNX COUNTERSPY	"Vigilant"
AIR FEUD	Wm. Hansbro
BURST TYRES	Alfred Edgar
SKID KENNEDY—SPEED KING	Alfred Edgar
THE SPY FLYERS	Capt. W. E. Johns
THE CRUISE OF THE CONDOR	Capt. W. E. Johns
BIGGLES OF THE CAMEL SQUADRON	Capt. W. E. Johns
BIGGLES FLIES AGAIN	Capt. W. E. Johns
THE CAMELS ARE COMING	Capt. W. E. Johns
THE BLACK PERIL	Capt. W. E. Johns
WINGS	Ed. by Capt. W. E. Johns
THE RAID	Capt. W. E. Johns
FOR VALOUR	Covington Clarke

THE ACE SERIES—*continued*

ACES UP	Covington Clarke
DESERT WINGS	Covington Clarke
ARNOLD ADAIR WITH THE ENGLISH ACES	
	Lt.-Col. Laurence Driggs
ARNOLD ADAIR WITH THE FRENCH ACES	
	Lt.-Col. Laurence Driggs
THE SECRET SQUADRON	Lt.-Col. Laurence Driggs
THE HORNET'S NEST	J. Railton Holden
WINGS OF REVOLUTION	J. Railton Holden
WINGS OF ADVENTURE	A. Whitehouse
THE COCKPIT: FLYING ADVENTURES	
	Ed. by Major C. H. Daniels
RHODES OF THE 94TH	F. Litten
VANDALS OF THE VOID	J. M. Walsh
FALCONS OF FRANCE	Nordhoff & Hall
PHANTOM WINGS OVER SPAIN	Eric Wood
REBEL SKIES	Eric Wood
SKYWAY AGENT	Eric Wood
WINGS OF HATE	Eric Wood
LONE STAR RANGERS OF THE AIR	Eric Wood
WINGED "MOUNTIE"	Eric Wood
WAR IN THE AIR	Major Helders
WINGS OVER AFRICA	David T. Lindsay
AIR BANDITS	David T. Lindsay
MASKED JUDGEMENT	David T. Lindsay
FLYING CRUSADER	David T. Lindsay
THE GREEN RAY	David T. Lindsay
WINGS OVER THE AMAZON	David T. Lindsay
THE FLYING ARMADA	David T. Lindsay
THE TEMPLE OF THE FLAMING GOD	David T. Lindsay
FLYERS OF THE NORTHLAND	John Allan
JUNGLE BIRDS	Charlton L. Edholm
WAR PATROL	A. S. Long
THE PIRATE AIRSHIP	John Noy
RED DEVIL OF THE AIR POLICE	John Noy
THE GREAT AIRWAYS PLOT	John Noy
WINGS OVER THE KHYBER PASS	F. E. Edsted

*These books can be obtained from any bookseller or
from the Publishers*

JOHN HAMILTON, LTD. (PUBLISHERS)
32 BLOOMSBURY STREET, LONDON, W.C.1